THE PARADISE JOB

A Selection of Recent Titles by Sally Spencer

OLD FATHER THAMES
SALT OF THE EARTH
UP OUR STREET

THE SALTON KILLINGS *

THE SILENT LAND *

MURDER AT SWANN'S LAKE *

* *available from Severn House*

THE PARADISE JOB

Sally Spencer

This first world edition published in Great Britain 1999 by
SEVERN HOUSE PUBLISHERS LTD of
9–15 High Street, Sutton, Surrey SM1 1DF.
This title first published in the U.S.A. 2000 by
SEVERN HOUSE PUBLISHERS INC of
595 Madison Avenue, New York, N.Y. 10022.

British Library Cataloguing in Publication Data

Spencer,   Sally,
          The paradise job
          1.   Bank robberies - Madeira Islands - Madeira - Fiction
          2.   Gangsters - England - London - Fiction
          3.   Detective and mystery stories
          I.   Title
          823.9'14 [F]

          ISBN 0-7278-5464-X

Typeset in Great Britain by Palimpsest Book Production Ltd
Polmont, Stirlingshire, Scotland.
Printed and bound in Great Britain by
MPG Books Ltd, Bodmin, Cornwall.

To Pepe and Marie, who have been very good friends for a long, long time.

Islands are rarely conducive to major crime, if only because the getaway is too difficult.

Berlitz Travel Guide to Madeira

Part One

Hook

A good plot, good friends, and full of expectation;
an excellent plot, very good friends.
Shakespeare: *Henry IV, Part One.*

One

Without a sawn-off shotgun in his hand, Frank Mason always felt vulnerable in banks. It was irrational, he knew, but every time the door swung open he half expected it to be the Old Bill, come mob-handed to haul him off. And in this particular bank, on this particular day, his normal discomfort was supplemented by a prickly heat which made his armpits itch.

He craned his neck so that he could see the front of the queue. With maddening slowness, the Portuguese cashier was counting out notes for a bald man with a mole on his head. Not much of a cashier. Not much of a bank, really. No bulletproof glass cages with recessed openings, just long unprotected counters. It reminded him more of the drapers' shops he had known as a boy.

The small child ahead of him was sniffing and complaining, and as his mother bent down to comfort him, she stabbed Mason's leg with the point of her parasol. It was the third or fourth time it had happened – Mason had lost count. The woman turned round, brushing her hair, sticky with sweat, under her straw hat.

"I'm most terribly sorry," she said. "It's Justin, you see. He's normally such a good little boy, but with all this heat . . ."

"Doesn't matter," Mason said gruffly.

The woman shrank away, intimidated, but it wasn't her he was annoyed with – it was Elsie. Elsie, who had suddenly decided in the middle of the day that she needed cash to go shopping with. Elsie, who, while he was roasting in this oven, would be sunning herself on their hotel balcony.

The man with the mole had finished his business and the queue shuffled forwards.

Mason hadn't wanted to come to Funchal at all. If he'd had his choice, it would have been a Scottish island. They had marvellous birds there, peregrine falcons, kestrels – even the names were magic. At that very moment he could have had his binoculars raised to his eyes, watching them ride the air currents, swooping and gliding with a grace that almost made him weep. The only birds he'd seen so far on Madeira had been bloody seagulls.

If he'd had the choice . . .

He wondered when he'd stopped having a choice. A sunny afternoon on Hampstead Heath seventeen years earlier, he decided. He had been lying on an old tartan rug, gazing at the sky, feeling at peace. Elsie had raised herself on to one elbow, looked down at him, and said shyly, "Well, what do you think, Frank? Shall we get married?"

He could have said no then, but she had looked so young and fragile, so much in need of protection, that instead he'd gone to see her father.

Ted Sims had received him in the front room of his new house in St John's Wood. He had stood perfectly still and serious, listening to Frank's bumbling declaration. When Mason had finished, Sims said, "You were nothing when I took you on, Frank. A petty criminal, just like your dad."

4

"I know that, Ted," Mason had replied, "and I'm very grateful."

Sims had smiled, showing off his newly capped teeth.

"I've never regretted it for a minute, Frank. You know why?"

Mason had shaken his head, although he was no fool and had a fair idea of the answer.

"Because you're tough, you've got nerves of steel, and you don't lose your head. We're taking on jobs now I'd never have thought about without you on the team."

It was true. The Sims Mob had always been held in wary respect, but since Mason had joined it, its reputation had grown and grown.

Sims had walked over to Mason and put his hand on his shoulder in an affectionate, prospective-father-in-law way.

"So what I'm saying is, even though my Elsie's still in her teens, if it's what you both want, then I've no objection. But remember Frank, we're Catholics."

The fingers tightened, digging into muscle and bone. Mason had reminded himself that for all that Sims, pushing fifty, no longer took an active part in the jobs, and despite the stylish clothes his new tailor was dressing him in, he was still a hard man. Hard – and ruthless – in a way that Frank could never bring himself to be.

"We believe that marriage is for ever," Sims continued, "so before you take the big step, think carefully."

He should have done – there was a choice – but he hadn't. Elsie was pretty and sweet and needed somebody to look after her.

Needed somebody to look after her! That was a joke. He'd started to find out just how helpless she was a couple of months before the wedding.

5

"I've booked the honeymoon, Frank," she'd said. "Two weeks in Brighton suit you? Course it will."

"Why didn't you ask me first?"

She'd smiled, but it hadn't been the soft smile he'd grown used to. There'd been something of a warning behind it, just the tiniest hint of a threat. For a moment, it was almost as if he were looking at her dad.

"Don't you worry your head thinking about planning things," she'd said. "Let's both stick to what we're good at."

The queue moved forward again, and Mason neatly side-stepped the prodding parasol. Another four people and he'd be at the front. It would be a relief to get out of the sticky atmosphere, even though the prospect of returning to his wife was far from attractive.

He'd been thinking of leaving Elsie for years, and the need had become even more pressing since he got involved with Linda. But there was so much standing in the way. For a start, Ted Sims was still around. Frank had never seen what he did to the competition – Ted had been too smart to try to push him into helping with that – but he had heard the stories and had no desire to be the main participant in the disappearing-kneecap trick.

Besides, he was not sure that he could manage without Elsie. In the early days it had been Ted who'd worked out all the jobs, but when he left the Sims Mob and started up on his own firm, it was Elsie who'd taken over that function. And much as it irked him to admit it, she was brilliant at her part. Which left him, at forty-two, as a combat veteran with little experience in planning and strategy.

But the main problem was money – he couldn't leave Elsie unless he had enough. He had been in the business for over twenty years, pulling one or two bank jobs a year. A fortune had passed through his hands, but what was left of it? A luxury flat with eleven years of the lease to run and a few thousand in the safety deposit box. He'd need to pull another job soon, and it was getting harder all the time.

'Nerves of steel,' Ted had said. Well that was then, in his twenties. He'd already served three years porridge, and found it a bloody sight easier to take than his early days in the East End. But that was a long way behind him now, he'd got used to the better things in life, and the prospect of a long sentence, even with time off for good behaviour, scared him to death. If he went inside now, he'd be an old man by the time he finally saw the light of day again.

He took out his handkerchief, and mopped his brow. It wasn't just the heat in the bank that was making him sweat.

What he needed, he told himself, was to make one big killing on his own. With money in his pocket, not Elsie's, he'd be free. He'd persuade Linda to leave that poncey spineless husband of hers – Nigel the Yachtsman! – and they'd be off and away. Australia or South America, where there were blue wrens, honey eaters and scarlet ibises. But could he ever pull a job off without Elsie? He'd had twenty years of being treated as the brawn. Maybe it was true, maybe . . .

The man two up in the queue from him did a crab-like scuttle, gurgled loudly as the breath was forced out of his body, and slumped to the ground. An epileptic! The people in the queue stood in stunned silence for a second, then bullied and pushed each other for the clearest view of the incident. Even the woman in the straw hat was there, Mason noted with disgust, shoving her little kid towards the front.

Placing his large hands on the nearest shoulders, he cleared a path to the fallen man. Nobody was doing anything, they were all just standing there and gawking. Mason knelt down and turned the man over so that he was lying on his back. His pupils were dilated and his face was turning black. Foam was forming at the corners of his mouth.

"Get me something to cover him," Mason ordered, "and a pillow. And get back – give the man room to breathe!"

There was an edge to his voice, an authority, which made the rubber-neckers obey.

Mason took out his plastic wallet of traveller's cheques and forced it between the man's teeth, to make sure that he did not bite his tongue. Someone handed him a blanket and a cushion. He laid the cushion under the man's head and draped the blanket on top of him and then held him, firmly but gently, through the shaking and juddering.

It did not take the fit long to run its course. The blackness drained from the victim's face, the pupils returned to normal.

"Where . . . what hap—"

"Just lie still," Mason said soothingly. "Get him a cup of tea, somebody."

He looked up to make sure that his instructions were being obeyed. The circle of watchers, made up of customers and bank employees, was keeping a respectful distance. Under Mason's gaze, one of the clerks detached himself from the group and headed towards the cafe across the street.

It was only when the bank officials, seeing that all the excitement was over, started to move back to their posts, that Mason realised that all of them – all of them – had come from behind the counter to look at what was happening. A minor crisis like this one and they had abandoned all sense of security!

And that was when he got the first glimmerings of his idea.

*   *   *

8

Mason walked along the sea front. The sun was blazing, but a tangy refreshing breeze blew off the water. His head felt cluttered. It was bit like having gas at the dentist's, the moment just before going under, when everything seemed weird and yet, at the same time, was starkly real.

He stopped in front of the harbour. There must have been well over a hundred boats moored there – fishing boats, small sailing craft, extravagant pleasure cruisers. A group of young people – little more than kids really – were stretched out on one of the decks, absorbing the heat. The girls wore skimpy bikinis; the boys tightly moulded, designer-label trunks. From their languid ease, Mason could tell that they had been brought up to expect this kind of existence.

"You don't know what real life's about, do you?" he asked them silently. "Well, good luck to you – and I hope you never have to find out."

The breeze built up, rattling the rigging around the aluminium masts. Seagulls circled and swooped, scavenging for food. Bloody ugly birds. Skilful, but not elegant.

"Like me," he said to himself.

He walked on to a promenade kiosk, a hexagonal cast-iron structure, painted green. It reminded him of the bandstand in the park, when he was a kid. He had gone to the band performances as often as he could; not to watch the band, although he envied them their immaculately pressed uniforms and brilliantly white shirts; nor to listen to the music, although sometimes it had been so overpoweringly beautiful that it had managed to cut its way even into his misery. He had gone there to look at the other children, out with their parents for the day, their small hands clasped reassuringly in larger adult ones – while he stood alone.

Mason sat down at a table next to one of the pillars, in the shade of the kiosk roof, and ordered himself a beer. He was just taking his first sip when the policeman appeared from nowhere. The cop was a tall man with blunt, serious features. On his hip was a leather holster. Mason froze for a second, then forced himself to say something.

"Excuse me, do you speak English?"

The policeman wheeled round on his heels to look at him.

"A leetle. Can I help you, senhor?"

Mason had been testing the water, and now he realised that he didn't know what to say next.

"That's your trouble, Frank," he told himself furiously. "You don't think. You don't plan ahead."

"Er . . . I just wondered if you'd heard the weather forecast."

The policeman smiled, and at once the image of a stern, armed guardian of law and order evaporated.

"Much sun, senhor," he said, "always much sun in Agosto."

The policeman resumed his saunter. Mason, who prided himself on being able to assess cops, had found no hint of suspicion or wariness in his eyes. More than that, he had detected none of the hardness that clung to the boys of the Met like an invisible shield. The Portuguese's toughness was no more than uniform-deep; he was a glorified traffic warden who would have no idea how to deal with a serious crime.

Mason turned his back on the sea and looked towards the edge of the town. He had read somewhere that Madeira was a volcanic island, the top of a huge mountain that had thrust its way out of the sea millions of years earlier. That would explain why there was virtually no flat land on the island, why even Funchal itself had been built on the slope leading to a peak.

10

He closed his eyes and conjured up a picture of the bank he had just visited and the narrow cobbled streets that lay around it. And suddenly, he had The Plan. There were details to consider, points to be cleared up, but the broad sweep of it was there, as if it had been nurtured somewhere else and planted, fully grown, in his brain.

He felt like a fish which had taken the hook and now had no alternative but to be dragged along by forces far superior to itself.

He paid for his beer and set off briskly back towards the hotel.

"Bugger it!" Elsie said to herself, as the false eyelash slipped from her tweezers and wafted down on to the dressing table.

She picked it up again, and painstakingly re-applied it. She had always taken trouble over her appearance – and it had paid off. She didn't really look any older than when she'd got married, just . . . well, more mature, more interesting. Frank hadn't changed much either, she admitted. He was still tall, dark and handsome, with his jet-black hair, broad nose and square chin. They looked good when they were out together.

Even so, she was bored with him. She didn't mind him not having a brain, that was one of the reasons why she'd chosen him in the first place. It was just that as she'd got older – more mature – she'd come to want somebody with a bit more . . . a bit more class.

The problem was her dad. He might still treat her like his little girl and give way to her on most things. But a divorce? Never!

There was a click, and she turned to see Frank standing in the doorway. She glanced at her watch, bought straight

11

after the last job. Fourteen hundred quid and worth every penny of it.

"You took your time in that bank!" she said.

"I've been hiring a car," Mason explained.

"You've what?"

"Been hiring a car. It's nice out. I thought we'd go for a spin."

That wasn't how she'd planned the day at all.

"I've got my shopping to do," she said.

"Shops don't close until seven. We'll only be out for a couple of hours."

"You paid a day's car hire for a two-hour run?"

"Bloody hell, Elsie," Mason protested, "you'll spend more than that in your first ten minutes in the shops."

True, and it was not the money that was bothering her. She didn't like Frank taking independent action – it might become a habit.

Mason moved over to the window. Elsie cocked her head to one side, and examined him closely, probably for the first time in months. He had that expression on his face that he assumed when he was trying to hide something. Usually it was nothing more than a sordid little affair, like the one he was having now with that slag Linda. But there hadn't been time for a woman that afternoon. Besides, how would that fit in with hiring the car?

He wasn't going to tell her, she could see that. He could be stubborn at times. Best to go along with him. He wouldn't be able to keep his secret from her for more than a few minutes. He wasn't bright enough for that.

"Yes, all right," she said. "Just give a minute to finish off my make-up."

*   *   *

12

The road from the hotel, past Santa Catalina Park, was relatively clear, but once they hit Avenida Arriaga the going became slow. A cruise ship had docked earlier, and the passengers rushed in and out of gift shops with scant regard for the traffic, anxious to spend as much money as possible in the short time they had. Lorries trundled up and down the narrow cobbled streets, squeaking and snorting as they braked to avoid pedestrians, roadworks or other parked vehicles.

"Those lorries shouldn't be allowed in the city centre," Elsie said. "It's not right."

"The drivers have got their job to do, like anybody else," said Mason, who was already incorporating traffic flows into his plan.

Elsie folded her arms, and glared with hatred at a tourist who was holding an expensive piece of embroidery up to the light.

"Well," she said, "I still don't think it's right. Somebody should do something about it."

The traffic thinned out as they turned on to the Rua 5 de Outubro, but by then they were being slowed down by the climb. Once out of the city, the surface deteriorated. The road was hacked out of the mountainside, and there was forest on their left and a steep drop on their right. Twice, they had to crawl behind ancient buses until there was an opportunity to overtake; three times Mason had to swerve to avoid trucks that were hurtling downhill.

"Disgraceful, I call it," Elsie said.

Even when they had a clear road, the steepness and the twists made it impossible for them to increase their speed much – ten miles from Funchal they had already climbed five thousand feet.

There were a few sidetracks leading up or down the hill, but

Mason did not turn off until the road that led to the Pico do Arieiro.

"Do you know where we're going?" Elsie demanded. "Or are you just guessing? Because if you think I want to be stuck . . ."

"We're going to the top of one of the peaks," Mason answered. "Five thousand nine hundred feet above sea level."

"Five thousand nine hundred feet above sea level," Elsie snorted, then added, with more interest, "in that case it should have a gift shop."

Mason risked a surreptitious look at his watch. Since they had left the town, they had managed to maintain an average speed of twenty miles an hour. In the early morning it should be quicker – but not that much quicker. Perfect!

There were no other vehicles on the road to the *pico*, just sheep. They munched grass on the verges and crossed from side to side with the same lack of care the shoppers had shown in Funchal.

The road came to an abrupt halt in front of a cafeteria. They got out of the car.

"I'm going to look at the view," Mason said. He pointed to the cafeteria. "Why don't you go in there and see if they've got any souvenirs?"

"Yes I . . . No," Elsie said. "I'll come with you."

She doesn't want to look at the scenery, Mason thought. It's me she's watching. I've only had the plan for a couple of hours, and already she's suspicious.

They stood for a while, Mason gazing down at the south side of the island and Elsie gazing up at him. The mountains gradually sloped down to green fields, and dotted between them were tiny hamlets in which the only buildings of any

14

importance seemed to be the white spired churches. The tourist brochure had called the island 'a semi-tropical paradise' and, for once, the copywriters hadn't been exaggerating.

You could pull a job in Manchester, Mason thought, and be on the M62 before the cops realised what had happened. And by the time they were properly organised, you would already be in your bolthole, an out-of-the-way farmhouse on the Yorkshire Moors or a flat you'd rented beforehand in Leeds. Then all you had to do was lie low for a few days until the heat died down. But here? Even if you managed to make it along the twisty roads to the other side of the island, there'd be nowhere to hide. In any of these villages a stranger would be noticed immediately.

"Not a very big place, is it?" Elsie asked, sniffing.

"Thirty-five miles by thirteen," Mason answered automatically.

"You seem to know a lot about it."

Elsie's voice was suddenly sharp – at least, sharper than usual. Mason cursed his carelessness.

"Read a guidebook while I was waiting in the bank," he said. "Let's go and look at the other side."

A sharply stepped track ran from the cafeteria down the side of the mountain. It reached a dip and then began to climb again, disappearing around the corner, but Mason had done his homework before hiring the car, and knew where it went from there. It was the hikers' trail, connecting the three highest peaks in Madeira and ending up at Santana on the north coast. Looking into the distance at the Pico Ruivo, he could just trace its continuation, a thin white band on the mountainside.

He moved on until he could see the whole of the southern side of the island. To his left were the fishing villages, sloping sharply down to the sea. Directly in front of him was Funchal: the large hotels; the houses clinging to the hillside, each with its own banana plantation; the docks and the marina. And to his left was the airport; a plane was just taking off, climbing sharply as it reached the edge of the short runway stretching out into the sea.

Robbing a bank in Madeira was a pushover, Mason thought. There was no security in the places themselves, and the police were totally unprepared. It was only a question of walking in and taking the money. Ah, but why was it so easy? Because once you'd carried out the raid, what the hell did you do then?

Hiding was impossible. Funchal wasn't that big, the police could turn the whole place over, calling in the army if they had to. And anywhere else, foreigners would stick out like sore thumbs.

Escape, then? There were only two ways off the island, by air and by sea, and within a few minutes of the hold-up both the harbour and the airport would be sealed off – and stay sealed off until the robbers were caught.

So escape was impossible too. The whole thing was impossible. Unless you had The Plan.

It was a more complex and ingenious scheme than anything Elsie had ever devised, an elaborate interconnection of checks and balances, relying for its success not just on physical force and timing, but on the psychological reactions of the opposition. It was a thing of beauty, a work of art, and he knew that he, its creator, would never rest until it had been carried out. Even the money didn't matter so much any more. He just wanted to pull it off.

Two

"Take a night flight, they said," Elsie complained as they cleared customs. "So what happens? We're two hours late taking off, and even when we get here the pilot keeps us circling for twenty-five minutes. It *was* twenty-five minutes," she said, as if Mason were about to challenge her, "I timed it."

"And what would you like him to have done?" Mason asked silently. "Ignore the control tower and land anyway, end up ploughing into the arse of another jumbo?"

Elsie always wanted things her own way – and she wanted them easy. He sometimes thought she saw it as a personal insult that the banks were making robbery so difficult. He penned a letter in his head. Dear Sir, We are planning to rob your establishment next Friday, weather permitting. If it rains, we would be grateful if you would post one hundred thousand quid in used notes to the above address. Thanking you in advance, Elsie Mason.

They negotiated their way through the milling hoard of red-eyed travellers. The luggage trolley squeaked, and there was something wrong with one of the front wheels, so that every few feet Mason had to jerk it violently to the right in order to keep it on a straight course. The cases were a bloody sight heavier coming back than they had been on the outward journey, too. Elsie had done herself proud in Madeira.

They had almost reached the exit doors when they saw the young man watching their approach. He had short brown hair which was expertly cut so as to make the best of the handsome, young-Robert-Redford face that it crowned. Looking at his earnest, intelligent expression, a casual observer might have taken him for a rising young executive. But as the eyes travelled lower, to the body encased in an expensive blue striped suit, the impression would have been dispelled. The body was hard, far harder than it could ever have become from afternoon squash sessions with the district manager. And there was something about the poise – the stance of the man – that suggested menace.

If Mason hadn't known him, he might have mistaken him for the Old Bill – it would not have been the first time they had followed him from the airport. As it was, he flung his arms around the young man in an affectionate – but definitely macho – embrace.

"Tony," he said, "what the bloody hell are you doing here at four o'clock in the morning? We could have got a taxi."

"Cab drivers around here are the biggest crooks in London," Tony Horton grinned. "Besides, it's always nice to have somebody welcome you home, isn't it?"

Mason noticed the look in Tony's eyes, and felt the customary warm glow followed by a stab of pain and disappointment. He had first seen that look seven years earlier when he had recruited Horton, then a callow youth, to do some minor work for him. And it was still there, even though Tony was now his trusted lieutenant, his right-hand man. Hero-worship! Because Mason was the toughest man

18

Tony had ever met, and even in early middle age could still take on all comers.

Mason was very fond of the younger man, too. Tony was his protégé, just as he himself had been Ted Sims'.

He had wanted kids when he'd got married, but Elsie had said she couldn't have any. He'd believed her at the time, but looking back on it, he was inclined to think that what she really meant was she didn't *want* them, and her infertility was just a screen to hide from her father the fact that she was on the pill.

All that was water under the bridge now. He supposed he'd come to regard Tony as a substitute son, even though there were only fifteen years between them. And he did like being looked up to, only . . . only he sometimes wished it was for something other than his muscle.

They walked between the rows of parked cars to where Horton had left his Porsche. The squeak of the trolley and click of Elsie's heels were overlaid with the gushing of water outside. Raining again, Frank thought. Well, what the hell had he expected?

Horton opened the back door for Elsie, and she climbed inside.

"Thank you, Tony," she said, just before he closed the door, "you're always such a gentleman."

The men went to the back of the car, and Tony unlocked the boot.

"If I was you," he said in a low voice as he handed Mason one of the leather suitcases, "I'd give Linda a call first thing tomorrow. She's been on the blower to me three times while you've been away. I think she's a bit pissed off about having to stay in the Smoke while you've been living it up in the sun."

"Living it up?" Mason demanded. Why was his life so dominated by demanding women? "I've been away with Elsie, for Christ's sake! Anyway, I've not just been frying my brains, I've been planning a job."

Ever since The Plan had come to him, he had been savouring the moment when he would tell Tony about it. He knew this was the wrong time, but he could hold it in no longer.

Tony chuckled.

"That Elsie," he said, with frank admiration, "never lets her mind rest for a . . ."

"Not Elsie," Mason said angrily. "Me!"

He realised he had raised his voice, and looked round the side of the boot at the car. He could see the back of Elsie's head, the tight permed curls, the gold earrings. She was looking straight ahead.

"I've been planning a job," he said again. "Elsie doesn't know about it. So for God's sake don't mention it to her."

He saw the doubt on his lieutenant's face. This was going to be even more difficult than he'd thought.

Linda Monk realised that she was fully awake, and no amount of fantasising about how she could entertain the entire Chelsea Football Club first team would send her off to sleep again. She sighed, switched on the bedside light, and reached for a cigarette. The smoke would probably irritate her husband and wake him up, but if he didn't like her bedroom habits, he could always move into the spare room.

Nigel grunted in his sleep, and she turned to look at him. The face, bathed in the pale yellow light, was that of a sandy-haired, weak-chinned boy. He hadn't altered since their marriage. What had changed, Linda thought, were his circumstances. She blew two angry jets of smoke down her nose, directly at the sleeping man. Nigel stirred, groaned again, and looked at his watch.

"It's half-past four in the morning," he said.

"I know it's half-past bloody four in the morning," Linda snapped back, "and I can't bloody sleep."

Nigel looked as if he were about to say something sharp, then a grin swept across his face.

"Well then," he said, squiggling his body so that he was closer to her, "since you can't sleep, old girl, how about a bit of the old nookey?"

His hand reached across for her breast, but she evaded him by slipping out of bed.

"I'm going to make some tea," she said.

She had always used sex as a weapon with Nigel. In the early days of their courtship, although she was no virgin, she had held it out as a future reward for marrying her, for lifting her out of her life of drudgery as a typist. Now she withheld it as a punishment for his failure to keep her in a lifestyle to which she had hoped to become accustomed.

The pokiness of the kitchen only added fuel to her anger. Nigel had seemed so glamorous at first, an ex-public schoolboy living on a private income, with a yacht moored in the Isle of Wight. She remembered standing on the deck, the wind blowing through her long hair, the striped sailor's T-shirt tight across her firm breasts.

She had been so clever to land him, so very clever. Except that soon after they were married, his father had died, leaving nothing but debts. The boat had gone, the flat had been sold, and they had ended up living in this rat-trap.

21

The kettle boiled and she poured the bubbling water on to the tea-bags.

"I say, old girl," Nigel called from the bedroom, "I wouldn't mind a cup myself."

She shouldn't have to do this sort of work. They should be able to afford a maid.

"No chance," she told herself bitterly.

Nigel made a kind of living as a free-lance photographer – bits of glamour work, the occasional celebrity profile. And odd long-distance shots of gentlemen out on the town with ladies other than their wives, photographs which the gentlemen in question seemed inordinately keen to buy off him. He even dabbled in stolen property now and again, fixing up deals to shift hot goods or arranging for the delivery of unregistered handguns. But it was strictly small-time stuff.

Not like Frank. Frank was into serious crime. He always had a lot of money – at least for the first few months after he'd pulled a job – and he was generous with it. She'd hidden all his expensive presents at first, but now she didn't bother. Let Nigel think what he liked. Frank was twice the man he was, in and out of bed.

"I said I wouldn't mind a cup myself."

"Get stuffed!" Linda said, banging a cup down with such ferocity that it shattered.

The brown liquid spilled on to the draining board, then trickled down to floor. She watched it, indifferently. She would clean it up in the morning. Or Nigel would.

She didn't love Frank, she wasn't even sure that she liked him very much. But then men weren't there to be liked, they were there to be used. And she wasn't getting full value out of him; the jewellery and clothes were all very well, but they

weren't enough. She'd better start putting pressure on him to
ditch Elsie and shack up with her. After all, he'd be burnt out
in a few years, and she wanted to be sure she'd still have her
looks when the time came to move on.

The Porsche moved speedily along the deserted London
streets, through South Kensington and into Knightsbridge.

Bloody good job that place is closed, Mason thought as
they passed Harrods, or Elsie'd want to stop and do a bit
of shopping.

At the end of the Brompton Road, Tony pulled the car
into a smooth turn, and they were home.

"Coming up for a drink?" Mason asked, trying to keep
any hidden meaning out of his voice.

Tony shrugged. "If it's not keeping you up."

It would have been just like Elsie to hang around, post-
poning the moment when Mason could unveil The Plan, but
for once she was co-operative. Maybe she was just too tired
to be bloody awkward.

"Thank you again, Tony, love," she said as she headed
for the master bedroom. "You're a real gentleman."

Tony gave Mason a wry look. It was Frank he owed his
loyalty to; the only part of Elsie he respected was her brain.
Mason mixed the drinks – a whisky for himself and a Bacardi
and Coke for Tony – and sat down on the leather sofa. The
sun was just rising, and through the picture window he could
see Hyde Park. Yet even as he relished the experience, he
remembered that the flat was on a short lease and the view
was only rented.

The two men made small talk until the taps had been
turned off, the loo flushed and Elsie was safely in bed.

"So, where's the job?" Tony asked finally, his voice edged

with doubt even before he'd heard the plan. "Local? Or up north?"

"Neither," Mason said. "Madeira."

"It's a big thing pulling a job abroad, Frank." The doubt had amplified. "Expensive. Will there be enough money to make it worthwhile?"

On that point at least, Mason was sure he could be persuasive.

"I want to pull it off at Christmas," he said. "There'll be thirty thousand tourists on the island then. And not people doing it on the cheap, like you find in Benidorm, you know. Me and Elsie went to the casino one night, and you've never seen so much money being thrown around outside Monte Carlo. They had three croupiers to each table, one to spin the wheel, the other two to rake the gelt in."

"Still," Tony said, "the casino's one thing but . . ."

"Thirty thousand tourists," Mason persisted, "and a hundred thousand locals, all wanting to splash out on the festivities."

"Even so . . ."

In a scrap, Mason thought, he'd follow me to hell and back. But when it comes to planning a job . . .

"Look," he said, "the banks usually close for the three days over Christmas, but this year, because Christmas Day falls on a Thursday, they'll be shut for five days. That means they're going to have a rush on the twenty-third, and they'll have to have a lot of cash to meet it, unless they want to run out and look like wallies. And there's only four or five main banks in the whole of Funchal. They'll be bursting at the seams."

"Shouldn't we ask Elsie what she . . ." Tony caught Mason's look and made a hasty amendment " . . .I mean, it's all very well pulling the job, but how do we get away?"

"Have you got a girl at the moment?" Mason asked. "Somebody you're sleeping with regular?"

"I've got one. I'm not shafting it at the moment, but it shouldn't take me much longer." He grinned at Mason's puzzled expression. "It's a virgin, this one, a barefoot orphan from up north. It just needs a bit more working on, that's all."

"Well, it'll be your choice," Mason said doubtfully, "but I'm not sure she sounds like the right sort for this job. Too much of a civilian."

"Christ," Tony said, "you're not thinking of taking women on the job, are you?"

"Oh yes, I am. They're an important part of The Plan."

Three

Raindrops drummed against the window, flattened and trickled down the glass. Mason watched them, each one doggedly pursuing a course it had not chosen, a course which would end, whether it willed it or not, where pane met wood. Did it ever do anything else but rain in England? he asked himself. After the job, before he finally settled somewhere, he would check up on the average rainfall figures.

He rolled over, nuzzling his nose in the pillow, and smelt the mixture of sweat and juices, that scent of animal sexuality which was peculiar to Linda. He could hear her now, brushing her long black hair in front of the dressing-table mirror — swish, swish, swish.

It wasn't much of a love-nest, this, he thought. The estate agent who had sold him the short lease had described it as a 'compact' flat – which meant bed-sit. Still, it had been all he was able to afford in this road populated mainly by respectable working-class West Indians and financially wobbly Yuppies.

The place had been decorated according to Linda's tastes – and God, it had cost. The walls were covered with embossed paper, the curtains were of heavy velvet. Shag-pile carpet covered the floor, and the bed, which dominated the room, was draped with a soft, fluffy counterpane. One thing you had to say about Linda: neither in her dress nor her choice of furnishings did she ever run any risk of being prosecuted under the Trades' Description Act.

He turned to look at her now. Her back was to him and her buttocks hung over the pink, woolly stool like a ripe peach. He could see the reflection of her breasts in the mirror, large and firm, by their very lack of sag defying the laws of gravity. A nice view but, like the one from his flat in Knightsbridge, only his as long as he had the money to pay for it.

As Linda brushed her hair, the breasts jiggled, and the two brown eyes in the centres of them stared at him invitingly. He was not tempted. He had yearned for her body on holiday, but that was before he had come up with The Plan, and even at the height of their passion that afternoon there had been a part of his brain that would not relax, that had been preparing itself for what he had to say now.

"I want you to do a job for me, darlin'."

She stopped brushing and froze. "What kind of job?" she asked suspiciously.

Linda was not keen on work, he thought, not unless she could do it on her back. But at least she didn't ask him if he meant that Elsie had a job for her, because, like most people, she didn't know that up till now – *up till now* – it had been Elsie who'd worked everything out.

"Don't worry," he said, "you'll like it. Two weeks in the sun and not much to do except get them glorious boobs a lovely shade of golden brown. Can't be bad. Right?"

Linda made a clucking sound to show her disapproval of his bad language. He wasn't fooled. At best her prudishness was only a vestige of her genteel, lower-middle-class upbringing in the suburbs. Now she was using it merely as a stall.

"Where?" she asked finally.

"Madeira." Mason reached over to his jacket, and extracted

the ticket he had bought that morning. "I've booked you on the night flight."

"You've just got back from there."

True, but how could he have done what was necessary with Elsie watching him? Besides, he admitted to himself, Linda, with her qualifications, was likely to be more successful than he would have been.

"You don't want Elsie to know about it, do you?" Linda asked.

She wasn't stupid, Mason thought, but then a stupid woman wouldn't be of much use to him.

"No," he said. "Elsie doesn't know. I'm doing the job for us. When I've pulled it off, we'll have enough money to go away." A thought struck him. "Does Nigel know about you and me?"

Linda shrugged her shoulders; her breasts bobbed rhythmically.

"He knows I'm carrying on with somebody," Linda said, "but I don't think he knows who. Why?"

"I think I might be able to use him as well."

"Same job?"

"No," Mason said quickly. "Something else I'm pulling on the side, to raise the seed money. So, what do you say to two weeks in Madeira?"

Linda started brushing again. She found a knot just below her left ear and, as Mason did his best to restrain his impatience, she began to untangle it. It seemed to take for ever. Mason lit a cigarette, not because he wanted one, just to give himself something to do with his hands – and still Linda's concentration was focused on her hair.

"Well, will you do it?" he demanded when he could restrain himself no longer, softening his voice to add, "I really need you on this one, darlin'."

28

"If you really need me," Linda said, "I want cutting in."

"For Christ's sake," Mason exploded. "I told you I was doing the job for us. What's mine's yours."

"And what's mine's yours, sweetheart," Linda said sincerely. "But if I'm going to be on the team, it's only right we get my share, isn't it?"

It made sense, Mason supposed. "You'll get the same cut as the shotgun men," he said. "Fair enough?"

He twisted his head to get a different angle on the mirror. Linda's lovely boobs disappeared and instead he could see her face. Her lips were curved in a smile of triumph.

"Fair enough," she said.

Although it was only late afternoon, Arnie the Actor was wearing a white dinner jacket and black bow tie. Today he was James Bond – Sean Connery not Roger Moore – and a Martini rested just next to the crisp, clean cuff of his dress shirt. Yesterday he had been Brendan Behan, and had stood, duffel-coated, knocking back the pints of Guinness until he fell over.

Robbie the barman had become an expert at spotting Arnie's *persona du jour* and could usually guess what drink to pour without being asked. He glanced at the bottle of Lamb's Navy rum on the shelf.

One day, he thought, one day he's bound to come clumping in here with a wooden leg and a bleeding parrot on his shoulder.

The door swung open and a young man in a sharp grey suit entered. Tony Horton.

Horton walked up to the bar, chose a stool two seats down from Arnie's, and ordered a rum and Coke. He wasn't, strictly speaking, a member of Crocket's, but Robbie wasn't about to refuse to serve one of Frank Mason's firm. Not that Frank was known to throw his weight around – but still . . .

It wasn't until he was well down his drink that Tony appeared to notice Arnie and ask if he'd like one. Twenty-four hours earlier, Arnie would have flung his arms around him and told him that he was the best friend a man ever had, then asked for 'a pint surr, if it wouldn't be too much trouble'. Now, he looked Tony coolly up and down and said in a deep voice, with just a trace of a Scottish accent, that he'd have a Vodka Martini.

"Shaken, not stirred?" Tony asked sarcastically.

Arnie, his eyes half-hooded, gave a slight nod.

Tony waited until Robbie had retreated to the other end of the bar, then said quietly, "Got any time on your hands?"

The corners of Arnie's mouth twitched into a sardonic smile, the smile of a man who knows he is about to be offered an almost suicidal mission, but who will accept it anyway, because only he can save the free world. He glanced quickly around the bar as if to make sure that Starlight Eddie, Kev the Shark and the other two or three regular afternoon boozers were not, in fact, SMERSH agents in disguise.

"What's the assignment?"

He really was a pain in the arse, Tony thought. Still it could have been worse – sometimes he thought he was Rasputin.

"I've got a friend who might be able to throw a bit of work your way," Tony said.

"That would be Frank Mason."

"Would it?" Tony said. He finished his drink. "It's best we're not seen together. I'm leaving now. Give it ten minutes and then follow me. I'll be waiting on the corner in a green Porsche."

"I drive," Arnie said. "You sit in the ejector seat."

Tony grinned. Well, you had to. "Just as you like," he said, heading for the door.

*   *   *

Nigel was sitting on the edge of the bed, playing with a rubber band stretched between his fingers and watching his wife pack.

"Look here, old girl," he said, "I'm not sure that I like the sound of this at all. I mean, what exactly does it involve?"

Linda held a dress up to herself and looked into the mirror. The neckline plunged, as it did on most of her summer clothes, almost to the navel. The hem was a little shorter than was fashionable, but then not many women had legs as good as hers.

"I've told you a thousand times," she said. "Mr Mason wants me to go and have a look at some property he's thinking of buying in Ma . . . the Canary Islands."

"Ma . . . ? You said, 'Ma . . .'"

"It was going to be Majorca at first, but he changed his mind."

She realised that in covering up her mistake, she had involuntarily clenched her fists, creasing the dress.

"Now look what you've made me do with all your questions," she shouted, stomping out of the bedroom, down the hallway and into the tiny kitchen.

She opened the cupboard door and the vacuum cleaner started to fall out. Furious, she pushed it back with her foot, while extricating the ironing board with one hand. While the iron heated up, she drummed her fingers impatiently on the board. The bedsprings creaked and she knew that Nigel had got up and was coming to join her. He appeared in the doorway.

"I mean, why you? What do you know about property?" His eyes narrowed. "He's not going with you, is he?"

"No," she said slowly, impatiently, as if explaining something to an extremely slow child. "He isn't. I met him in the

Orinoco Club a couple of times and we got talking. He wants to buy some flats and he doesn't want his wife to know about it. And if he uses one of his regular staff, she'll be bound to find out."

"Staff!" Nigel said. "Staff! It's not a businessman you're talking about, it's a gangster – a thug."

"At least he's a man of some kind," Linda said.

She spat on the iron. It sizzled. She placed the dress on the board and began to smooth out the wrinkled patch.

"Look, if you'd like to come with me, to make absolutely sure I'm going on my own, then you can," she said. Nigel looked at her with sad, hopeful eyes, like a dog which has been offered a bone. Even his ears seemed to prick up, but they dropped again instantly when she added, "Provided, of course, you've got the money."

"You know I haven't," he said. "Most of what I earn goes to clothe you."

Linda ran her tongue around the edges of her mouth as she concentrated on making a perfect crease.

"Well there you are," she said. "You can't expect Mr Mason to pay for you as well, now can you? So you'll have to stay at home."

His lip curled – the small boy who has been hurt and wants his nanny to comfort him. She softened a little.

"You might be flush again soon," she said. "I've put in a good word for you with Mr Mason. He's got a job he wants doing."

"What does he want? Some photographs taken?"

What *did* he want? What possible use could Frank have for a weed like Nigel?

"I don't know what the job is," she said. "He didn't tell me, did he?"

Nigel was nibbling at his lower lip. Even the thought of working for Frank was making him nervous.

"Is it legal?" he asked.

Oh, for God's sake! It really was pointless trying to be nice to him. "I shouldn't think so," she said. "Who the hell would employ you to do anything legal?"

Nigel carried Linda's suitcases down to the front door and watched until the cab – paid for by 'Mr' Mason – had disappeared round the corner. He had suspected for some time that Linda was having an affair. Now he was sure that she was, and that her lover was Mason.

He couldn't blame Linda in a way. She was a mercenary little bitch, but he'd known that when he married her. Her dowry was her body, his money the bride-price. She had held to her side of the bargain, she was as beautiful as she had ever been – but he hadn't been able to keep up his.

All his problems had one simple solution – money. If he became rich, Linda would come back to him soon enough. And though whatever job Mason offered him wouldn't pay that much – who *would* pay him that much? – there might be a way to put a squeeze on the gangster for more. Getting the money from Mason rather than anyone else would be doubly sweet; he might not be brave enough to fight his wife's lover, but there were other ways in which honour could be served.

Arnie was James Bond when he came through the door, but as he walked across the room to where Mason was standing his shoulders drooped, the sardonic expression was replaced by world-weariness, and he was transformed back into what he really was – a two-bit actor who had never made the big time. Mason had seen the change many times. The property tycoon who couldn't handle the deal himself because it would only force the prices up, the MoD Weapons Export Officer in temporary financial difficulties, the captain of the supertanker who could lay his hands on thousands of barrels of oil dirt cheap – all these characters disappeared once the mark had been dropped off at his hotel. Yet each time insignificant little Arnie emerged from the shell of his creation, Mason was both amazed and disappointed, as if he had hoped for a while that the actor had finally managed to escape from the trap in which he was caught.

But none of us can, Mason thought, not without money.

"Sit down, Arnie," he said, indicating one of the dinky pink easy chairs that Linda had insisted on buying. "Sorry about this place. I know it looks a bit like a Port Said brothel, but at least it's private. Right?"

"Absolutely," Arnie replied. The rich, modulated voice was not put on. That at least, he could call his own.

"I'm pulling a bank job in three or four months," Mason said, "and I want you to help set it up for me."

Scams were Arnie's line, bank jobs were a bit out of his depth. But you didn't just turn somebody like Frank Mason down out of hand. Arnie tried to will James Bond back to help him with his problem, but the secret agent had gone into hiding.

"Why me?" he asked, his deep voice coming out slightly choked.

"Two reasons," Mason said. "One, we need a con man to make this work." He saw that Arnie, despite his nervousness, was scowling. "Sorry, Arnie, not a con man, a what-do-you-call-it, thespian."

Arnie nodded.

"You'll have to visit the place," Mason continued. "Don't worry, you'll be away long before we hit the bank. The second

34

thing I want is somebody who knows all the faces – who can get me a team together. You'll be a sort of recruiting sergeant."

Arnie looked at Tony, who was still standing by the door. "I thought he did that."

"Normally, yes," Mason agreed. "But this one has to be top-bleeding-secret. I don't want anybody outside the team getting even a whiff of what's going down. Money: I take twenty per cent plus operational expenses off the top, and the rest is divided up equally. It should be a big haul." He leaned forward until his face was almost touching Arnie's. "If you want to, you can leave now, but if you stay, and I tell you all the details, there's no backing out. Think about it."

Arnie did think about it. The idea of violent crime scared him, even though, as far as he knew, Mason's firm had never actually hurt anybody. His wisest move would be to leave while he had the chance. On the other hand, Mason had always been big-time, and this robbery seemed bigger than most. With his share, he could set up his own theatre company. He gulped. "I'm in."

"Christmas," Mason said. "Madeira. We don't know which bank yet, but we will soon."

"But that's an island," Arnie said. "How are you going to get away?"

Mason's eyes suddenly became cold and hard. "You'll be well away yourself by then, Arnie," he said, "so that's not your bloody problem, is it? You just do your job, and leave all the thinking to me. Right?"

As he spoke, he jabbed a thick heavy finger in the actor's direction, emphasising each point.

He could finish me off with that finger alone, Arnie thought. He had not seen Mason for a while, and had forgotten just how tough he was. Now he remembered the night in The

Duke of Clarence – the football hooligans with the broken bottles in their hands – and he shuddered. "Right!" he said. "No offence, Frank."

"None taken," Mason said. "Just remember what I said, and we'll get on. I want you to recruit a team, a bit tricky this one, because I don't want anybody I've ever used before. Look round, see who's available, then check back with me and . . ."

Mason always used a team of four. Himself, Tony . . .

"You'll need a driver and one other shooter," Arnie interrupted.

"You're thinking again, Arnie," Mason said menacingly. "I'll tell you what I want. I need three shooters and a driver."

"Christ!" Arnie said in spite of himself, "must be a bloody big bank. I mean . . . sorry, Frank."

"And one of the shooters," Mason said, "must be a married man who's just done time for armed robbery."

Was this some kind of joke? Arnie asked himself. Anybody who'd just done bird for a stick-up would have served at least an eight-year stretch. Some of them recovered, but a lot were never the same again. Why, when there were so many young men who'd give their right arms to work with Frank Mason, did he want an old lag? He looked at Mason's face, desperately searching for a flicker of humour, and found none. He wished to Christ he'd walked out while he'd had the chance.

"There's one other person I definitely want on the team," Mason continued, "Portuguese Pedro."

That was even worse than the idea of the ex-con. Arnie was frightened of arguing with Mason, but he was frightened of going to jail, too.

"He's nothing but a gas-meter bandit," he said. "What the hell do you want to use him for?"

"They speak Portuguese in Madeira. Right? Portuguese

Pedro speaks Portuguese. Right? So we need him. There's no point in threatening people with shotguns if the buggers can't understand what you're saying."

Arnie glanced longingly at the door, and at Tony Horton blocking it. His stomach was turning to water, but he knew he had to press on.

"But Portuguese Pedro! The man's a no-count, a loser. He'll be a liability on the job. Let me look around, Frank," he pleaded, "see if I can come up with anybody else who speaks Portuguese."

"I want Pedro," Mason said firmly, "and I don't want any bloody arguments. Right?"

Arnie's heart was thumping in a way it never did when he was pulling a con. His own line of work was logical, and he was always in control. Now he seemed to have fallen into the hands of a lunatic. He looked up at Mason's face. That seemed normal enough, no crazy flashing eyes, no maniacal twist of the lips, just a hard, immovable blankness. His gaze fell down to the other man's powerful knuckles which he knew could pulverise him in a matter of seconds. He forced himself into one last desperate attempt to make Mason see reason.

"You're the boss, Frank," he said. "No question. Only . . . only it looks like you're planning a deliberate disaster."

For a moment, under Mason's stony gaze, he thought he had gone too far. Then the other man's expression changed and his lips formed, not a mad smile, but a normal, rational, amused grin.

"Yes," Mason said. "It does, doesn't it?"

Four

Her name was Susan. She reminded Mason of the girls in the shampoo advertisements; the ones whose faces are young, pretty and, above all, innocent, and who run barefoot across cornfields, their dresses billowing around them.

"I've got to slip out for twenty minutes," Tony had told her after he'd brought the drinks at the bar. "You don't mind, do you? Frank'll keep you amused."

And with that, he'd gone – as arranged.

"Tell me about yourself, darlin'?" Frank said.

"How d'you mean, Mr Mason?"

She had a nice voice – soft, warm.

"Just your background. Where you're from. What you're doing in London."

She smiled, puzzled but not suspicious. "What's this all about, Mr Mason?"

"Call me Frank," Mason said. "What's Tony told you about this holiday?"

"That it's abroad, somewhere hot, and that you want me to . . . to tell a lie to the police."

"Not a lie," Mason said. "We just want you to refuse to tell the truth for a while. So, if I think you're suitable, we'll be giving you a holiday, all expenses paid, just for keeping your mouth shut for a few hours. Don't

38

you think we're entitled to know a little bit about you first?"

"I . . . I suppose so," Susan said. She looked into his eyes. Her own were wide, doe-like. "I'm from the north and I'm twen . . . nearly twenty-one."

Half my age, Mason thought.

"And why did you decide to come down to the Smoke? Looking for a new job?"

"I never had a job before I came to London," she said. "Me dad died when I was little, so there was just me and me mam. She's never been what you might call well, and for the last few years she needed constant nursing."

"She's dead now, is she?" Mason said, sympathetically.

Susan nodded, and a small tear fell from the corner of her eye, landing on the formica tabletop.

"It was for the best, really, she was in a lot of pain. Anyway, after she died, I couldn't stand Accrington. Everything about it seemed to remind me of her. So I came here."

"And do you like London?"

"It's all right, Mr Mason . . . Frank. I mean, it's a bit of a struggle. By the time I've paid for me digs, there's not much left over for luxuries," she smiled again, a self-deprecating grin, "like food. And until Tony came along, I hadn't got any friends. I suppose it's me own fault really, I've not had much practice in making them, not with having to look after me mam."

Poor little sod, Mason thought.

Her eyes flashed with anger, as if she had read his thoughts.

"Not that I'm blaming her," she said. "Me mam was very brave."

"How did you meet Tony?"

"He came into the newsagent's where I work. He was very nice, very kind. We started going out together." ·

Mason chuckled involuntarily at this description of the relationship. *Going out* was the last thing Tony had in mind when he picked up a girl.

The delicate brown freckles on Susan's nose were suddenly swamped in a sea of redness. She lowered her eyes to the table and with her index finger began to draw lines from a puddle of beer.

"I'm not cheap, Mr Mason," she mumbled. "Tony's the first real boyfriend I've ever had. I don't let everybody . . . I'm not a common . . ."

"I know you're not, darlin'," Mason said, ashamed of himself.

She looked up, smiling gratefully, then her face became earnest again.

"Mr Mason," she said, "I really need this holiday. I hope I've not said anything that might disqualify me."

"We'll talk about it again when I've seen Tony," Mason said. He looked at her, this serious young woman in a cheap worn dress, and reached for his wallet. "Here's a hundred quid," peeling off the notes, "get yourself some decent clobber."

She shook her head.

"Come on, darlin'. You'd have the holiday in Mad . . . you'd have the holiday. How is this different?"

"I'd be earning that. Oh, I know you claim there's nothing to it, but if it's costing you that much, it won't be easy. D'you know what we say in Lancashire?"

"No."

"You don't get owt for nowt."

"Have the money," Mason urged. "I can afford to give it to you."

"I know that," Susan said quietly. "But I can't afford to take it."

"You're a bit of a bastard, aren't you?" Mason said, as he pulled up at the traffic lights on Kensington Road.

"Why?" Tony asked. He seemed surprised, and a little offended.

"That girl, Susan. She's a nice kid. What made you pick her up in the first place?"

"There's something special about unbled meat," Tony said. "It's very willing, and it does what you tell it, even if it doesn't fancy the idea itself."

Mason glanced at his lieutenant, and saw a leer on his face. When had this begun to happen? When had the fresh-faced lad who'd first joined the firm changed into this experienced – what was the word? – roué? Mason felt like a father who, still expecting his son to be interested in model railway magazines, finds a *Penthouse* hidden under his mattress.

The lights changed, and he eased the car forward.

"I told you at the beginning I didn't think she was right for this job," he said, "and now I'm sure of it. Once the shit hits the fan, the women will be under a lot of pressure. It'll be all right for the others, they're tough and they've been brought up to it, but it could hurt her. She's so . . . innocent."

"That's why she's so perfect," Tony said gleefully. "The police will never believe that anybody could be that naive. They'll put all the pressure on her, and leave the others alone. And don't underestimate her, Frank. She may not be very bright, but she's stubborn. If she's promised us she'll do it, she'll keep her mouth shut for a long time."

"She'll crack in the end," Mason said.

41

The endless hours of interrogation, the same questions over and over again, the feeling of isolation – and the way the police played on it – would break anyone but the toughest man. Who knew what damage it could do to the girl?

"Of course she'll crack in the end," Tony said. "That's the beauty of it. When she does crack, what's she got to tell them? Nothing except what we want them to know anyway!"

Mason signalled, and overtook a tourist bus unloading a few dozen eager, camera-swinging Japanese at the entrance to Hyde Park. He turned down Sloane Street.

Just what kind of mind had Tony developed?

"I thought we were going back to your place," Horton said.

"I've changed my mind," Mason replied. "I fancy a trip south of the river. Listen, Tony, I really don't want to use her."

"Well, I do," Horton replied, and there was a dangerous edge to his voice. "You said it was up to me, and she's the one I want."

They were inches away from a fight, Mason realised, one that had nothing to do with Susan at all – at least not directly. He had treated Tony like a growing son over the years, gradually giving him more and more responsibility until the young man had become his second-in-command. And now he was playing the stern father, pulling the rug from under Tony, telling him that he didn't trust his judgement. And the judgement was right – it was a clever plan to use the girl. It just didn't feel right.

He couldn't afford to antagonise Tony, not at this stage of the operation, not when everything was so delicately balanced.

"I'll tell you what," he said. "You try and get another woman – try really hard, Tony. But if you don't find one, then it's Susan. Fair enough?"

"Fair enough," Horton said.

If the police really put her through it, he would see that she was well compensated. He'd give her a few thou out of his own cut. She could leave the dingy boarding house they'd dropped her off at, and could get somewhere decent. And buy some new clothes. For a few hours' discomfort, he'd be giving her more money than she could earn in a couple of years. That was a fair trade – wasn't it?

For the second time since he'd met the girl, Mason felt ashamed.

"I used to live there," Mason said, pointing across the wasteland to the billboard announcing the imminent construction of a block of flats. "Right there, just under the word 'luxury'."

Tony merely grunted noncommittally.

Well, he didn't know what to say, Mason thought. Brought up on the 'good' side of Greenwich, he had no idea what it had been like to be a kid in this district. The corner shops, the narrow streets, the decaying houses – memories.

Dad, coming home from the pub, his breath sour with alcohol, his face creased with frustration and disappointment. Dad, swaying with the drink, looking down at his young, half-starved son and saying, "I'll teach you, you little bastard."

Teach him what? What had he done? And then the beating. Maybe in other homes the father actually did strip off his leather belt and lay in with that, but Spike Mason

could never wait that long – it was the flat of his hand if
Frank was lucky, fists if he wasn't.

Mum, shaking him roughly as he lay shivering in his
bed on cold winter nights and saying, "You'll have to get
up. Your Uncle Reggie's here, and he wants to lie down for a
bit."

Uncle Reggie? Uncle Charlie, Uncle Walter, Uncle
Stanley . . . a succession of men who had a few quid in
their pockets, felt like a shag, and knew Peggy was always
willing to oblige.

"Why do I come back?" Mason asked himself.

Because this was also the neighbourhood in which he'd
joined Ted Sims' gang, gradually becoming a respected
figure, a man to be reckoned with. And that was still
true. However much he felt his life was a failure, however
much he considered that he had taken the wrong turn and
was now trapped by the consequences – driven down the
narrow tunnel of crime from which there was no escape –
he was still regarded as one of the area's success stories.
And now and again, on days like today, he felt the need to
be looked up to.

Mason was surprised to find, among this blight of urban
decay, that Spooner's Snooker Hall was not only still
standing, but even appeared to be open.

"Fancy a quick game?" he asked.

Tony said he didn't mind.

Mason opened the door.

"Watch the steps," he advised. "There's three of 'em."

The place hadn't changed at all; the same barn of a room,
gloomy apart from the brilliant lights over the tables, the
same peeling green paint and flyblown notices. The same
old Greasy Spooner too, standing in front of the refreshment

counter, his bony elbows sticking out of the holes in his knitted green cardigan – and he'd been older than God when Mason was a lad.

Frank walked over to the counter. Faded cardboard signs advertised cigarettes the tobacco companies had long since ceased making. The milk machine whirred erratically, its central propeller hardly stirring the yellowing liquid that surrounded it. The box of Durex, which Greasy used to keep under the counter, was now on open display, but looking at the packets it seemed likely that all the rubbers were well past their shag-by date.

He took a five-pound note out of his wallet.

"Give me some change, Greasy."

"Right, Frank . . . er . . . Mr Mason," Spooner said, diving for the wooden cash drawer. "We . . . er . . . don't often see you round here nowadays."

People in this neighbourhood were never sure whether to treat him like a long-lost friend or a visiting superstar. Mason grinned good-naturedly. "You know how it is, Greasy. Been busy."

The hall was empty except for five young lads, all dressed in sleeveless jean-jackets, who were crowded round the far table.

Just like in my day, Mason thought, except that back then they'd have been wearing cheap snazzy suits.

But their motive would be the same as his generation's. Snooker was not only a way of killing time: it offered them a chance, a slight one, of being the next Hurricane Higgins, of an escape from poverty and tedium.

Not all the kids were intent on their game. The biggest, a lad of twenty-two or twenty-three, was watching him – and had been ever since Greasy had said his name.

Mason took the break, and left a shot on. Tony potted four reds, three blacks and yellow before his inexperience began to tell and he found that not only had he set nothing up for himself, but he was in danger of leaving the game wide open for his opponent. He tried a snooker, and it didn't work.

"Don't worry about it, my son," Mason said, slapping him on the shoulder. "You haven't had the practice, that's all. Disadvantage of a privileged upbringing. Right?"

He was a good player, and Tony had made it easy for him. He potted the reds with style and assurance. It was only when he reached the colours that he realised he was the only one playing. The boys on the other table had given up their own game and were standing by the left-hand top pocket, watching him.

Everything went smoothly until the pink, then he miscalculated the angle and was left with the cue ball lying wrongly. He could still pot the black, but it would be awkward – off the side cushion and into the top right-hand pocket. Thinking about the shot, he slowly chalked his cue.

"Ooo," a mock-pansy voice called out, "he's putting on his mascara."

Mason bent over the table, lined up the black and took the shot. The cue ball struck and stopped almost dead, as he'd intended it to. The black hit the cushion and rebounded. It slowed as it approached the pocket – he'd had to do it that way – teetered on the lip, and then fell in. It was a good shot and Mason was proud of it.

"Bloody rubbish!" said the same voice as before, but this time with a vicious edge to it.

Mason placed the balls back on the table and began to fit the reds into their wooden frame. A pair of strong hands, palms down, appeared on the table. Mason's eyes travelled up thick, tattooed arms, past broad shoulders, to a face. The lips were thick, the teeth badly cared for; the nose had once been broken and the eyes blazed with anger.

"So you're Frank Mason," the young man who had been looking at him earlier said.

"That's right, son," Mason said easily. "Now if you'll take your arms off this table, we can carry on with our game."

"Big tough Frank Mason," the other sneered.

He reached across, lifted the wooden triangle, and scattered the balls all over the table.

Mason had met this before, local hard-cases wanting to chance their arms against the famous gangster. He understood it. A reputation was all they could hope for, their only ticket to self-respect. He had been like that himself. *Had been?*

The boy with the broken nose was less than three feet away from him. Mason didn't look, but he knew – because that was how he had survived so long – that the other four had not moved from their position near the top left-hand pocket. But they would not stay there for long, not if there was aggro.

"What's your name, son?" he asked.

"Denny," the broken-nosed boy said, sounding surprised.

"Well look, Denny," Mason said, "I don't want any trouble. I just want a quiet game of snooker. Why don't you walk away and we'll forget the whole thing."

"Better do what he says," Greasy called out nervously from the safety of his counter.

Denny backed away a little.

"Big tough Frank Mason," he said again. He seemed to like the line.

He was fast, but crude. By the time his right arm was in the air, his body had already signalled to Mason exactly what to expect. Frank blocked the blow, jabbing forward with his own right at the same time.

Denny was in shape, but it would have taken a brick wall to resist the force of Mason's fist. He started to slump forward, the air making a whooshing sound as it was forced out of his mouth. His knees had hardly had a chance to bend when Mason followed through to his chin, and his neck whip-lashed back. His body hung there uncertainly, not knowing which way to fall, which blow to react to. Mason helped it make a decision by kicking him in the crotch – with four more to deal with, there was no time for niceties.

Well before Denny had hit the ground, Mason was ready for the next attack. The louts had split up, two going for Tony over by the scoreboard, two for him. Tony waited until the first was almost in range, then swung his cue. It whistled through the air in a tight arc, catching the boy in the throat. His eyes were suddenly wider, his tongue hung out, and, gurgling, he sank to his knees.

One of Mason's attackers was coming around the table, the other across it. The one on the baize would get there first. He ducked his head to avoid the heavy overhead light cover just a split second after Mason had swung it. The edge caught the side of his skull, there was a loud crack, and he somersaulted backwards.

The second boy, covering the distance by a longer but safer route, was almost there. He feinted a kick and brought his head down to butt Mason. But his target had already moved, and his head cut through empty air, only stopping when his nose was cracked by Mason's upswinging fist.

Mason went in low, grabbing with one hand the collar of his tee shirt, with the other his testicles, and lifting him off the ground.

"Me balls!" the boy screamed. "Leggo of me balls!"

He got his wish. Mason flung him down again on the still-recumbent Denny.

Frank turned his attention to Tony's problems. The one he had hit with his cue was still down. The other, his face covered with blood, was cowering against the wall while Tony systematically pounded at him.

"Enough!" Mason shouted to his lieutenant

Tony stopped immediately, and the boy collapsed.

Mason bent down, searching among the tangled arms and legs for Denny's head. The young thug had lost a couple of teeth, his mouth and nose were bleeding, and one eye was already puffing up.

"Can you hear me, son?" Mason asked.

Denny nodded his head.

"If I was you," Mason said softly, "I'd take my mates and get out of here as soon as possible."

The boy groaned.

"Yes sir, Mr Mason," he finally managed to utter, "I'll do that."

It was five minutes before they were in any state to leave, then they hobbled out, supporting each other as best they could. Mason watched their progress with sorrowful eyes — sorrow for them, sorrow for himself. It was always going to be like this, there'd always be someone who wanted to challenge tough Frank Mason. Except that as the years went by, he'd find it harder and harder to live up to his reputation.

The Madeiran job had to work!

*   *   *

Each step on the stairway up to the bed-sit in Matlock Road had seemed a mile high, but coming down again Portuguese Pedro felt like he was floating.

This was how he had imagined it would be in the old days, back in his home village in the mountains near the Spanish frontier. Week after week, he had sat in the cinema with the other farm boys, smelling of cow dung no matter how hard they scrubbed themselves, and marvelled at the life led by gangsters in London and Chicago – the cars, the women, the money. If only he could get there, he had told himself, he would soon be king of the underworld.

And so, one night when his parents were sleeping, he had crept quietly into their room, reached under the bed, extracted the box that contained their life savings, and left the village for ever.

It had not been long before harsh reality had forced him to realise that he was strictly small fry, a robber of sub-post-offices and mugger of old-age pensioners. But he had never stopped yearning for what might have been, if he'd had the chances – if he'd been an entirely different person.

When Arnie the Actor had told him that Frank Mason wanted to see him, his first instinct had been to run. What could a man like Mason want with him? What had he done to offend someone so powerful? He had entered the bed-sit like a nervous dormouse.

He reached the bottom of the stairs, opened the door, and stepped out into Matlock Road. The air, for once, tasted wonderful. The chirping of the birds was a symphony of triumph.

He could remember every word that Mason had said to him.

"We've been watching you very carefully, Pedro, and we think you're ready for the big time. We're going to pull a bank job and we need a key man. Are you interested?"

Interested? Pedro had nearly fallen to the ground and kissed Mason's shoes. Frank Mason was offering him a place on his team! He'd have done the job for nothing.

"The job will be in two or three months. I can't give any details yet – not even to you, Pedro."

Not even to you, Pedro. Wonderful words, intoxicating words. Pedro strutted along the pavement.

A middle-aged black woman, heavily laden with Sainsbury's carrier bags, was approaching him. Pedro kept straight on course, and the woman stepped to one side. He had only been on Mason's team for ten minutes, and already people could sense his power!

Mason watched him from the upstairs window. "'Where we do it, Meester Mason?'" he mimicked. "'When we do it, Meester Mason?' He's just like a kid queuing outside a strip show and pretending he's not got a hard-on. 'You won' regret it, Meester Mason. I do a good job, Meester Mason.'"

"What a wally," Tony Horton said.

The pub on Kilburn Lane was what Mason called an ODB – ordinary decent boozer. The bar was doglegged and a brass railing ran round the bottom of it because, as every competent landlord knows, it is impossible to drink a pint properly unless one foot is four inches higher off the ground than the other. The barmaid was red-haired and freckled, with the kind of smile that almost forces men to tell her that their wives don't understand them. The canned music sounded like American Country and Western, although

51

the singer kept repeating that he wished he 'was back in Oireland'.

The frosted door swung open, and Linda entered. She was wearing a white dress that contrasted perfectly with the gold of her skin – and there was a lot of that on view. The dress looked new, and probably was. Mason supposed he could charge it to expenses when they divided the loot.

She smiled at her lover, then looked around in disgust. Mason grinned. This wasn't her sort of place at all, she was more for bars with subdued lighting where they served peculiar-coloured drinks with little paper umbrellas sticking out of them.

He led her to a table in the corner, far enough away from the other drinkers to avoid being heard. "Gin and tonic?" he asked.

Linda grimaced. "Madeira."

Silly cow! The pub didn't have it, of course, and she settled, rather ungraciously, for a sweet sherry.

"So how did you make out?" Mason wanted to know.

"I had a really good time," Linda said.

She was teasing him, like she did in bed. But that was a good sign, because when the teasing was over, she always delivered the goods. He sat back and waited.

"I was very clever," she continued. "I told them in the hotel that I wanted to make a money transfer, and asked which bank I should go to. They said the hotel uses the Banco de Lisboa."

It was in the Rua do Aljube. Mason remembered it well. Black, smoked-glass windows, door in the middle of the frontage. One way street. Narrow lanes running off every hundred yards or so.

"But do the other hotels use it?" he asked.

The job would be expensive to set up in the first place, and his share of the haul had to be enough to last for ever. The bank they hit had to be a big one.

"I'm coming to that," said Linda the teaser. "I went down to the bank, and I made a real mess of cashing my traveller's cheques. At first I couldn't find them, then I dropped them on the floor, then I signed them in the wrong place."

"Get on with it," Mason snapped, but Linda only smiled.

"By this time, there was a big queue behind me, and the cashier told me to hurry up. That was what I was waiting for. I screamed the place down, said I'd never been so insulted in my life, and demanded to see the manager."

"And did you?"

"No, but I got to see the Chief Cashier, which was better."

"Why?" Mason asked.

"Well, I expect the manager would have been a grey-haired old man, but the Chief Cashier was still quite young. And you know I get on better with younger men, Frank. Anyway, he took me out for a coffee, and within five minutes he was telling me all about the bank."

"You didn't ask too many questions, did you?" Mason asked anxiously. "I don't want them getting suspicious."

Linda crossed her legs and leant forward. The front of her dress pulled tightly against her breasts, fighting hard to hold them in. For a moment, it seemed like it would lose.

"I didn't ask him *any* questions," she said. "He just came out with it all. I think he wanted to impress me. And Frank, listen. Not all hotels bank with the Lisboa, but most of the big ones do. So do a lot of the other businesses in Funchal, gift shops, restaurants, places like that."

"You seem to have learned a lot over one cup of coffee," Mason said.

Linda looked vaguely uncomfortable. "Well no, actually," she said. "Most of it came out later. He invited me out to dinner, you see. That's when he told me."

Mason didn't believe her. That kind of indiscreet bragging was more common in bedrooms than restaurants. He should be angry, he told himself. He should feel betrayed. But he was honest enough to admit that he'd sent Linda rather than Tony because he knew she'd use her charms to get the information. It was her uninhibited sexuality that was her main appeal – and you couldn't expect a racehorse not to run when it had the chance.

"And what have you been doing while I was away?" Linda asked, getting off the subject. "Seen Nigel yet?"

"No," Mason said. "I haven't had time to get round to it."

Linda's eyes narrowed. "You never did say exactly what you wanted him to do, did you?"

"No," Mason said. "I didn't. But I've told you it's nothing to do with the operation." He was not a very good liar, not with Linda, and he knew it. "And I don't want you talking to him about it," he continued. "You just keep your mind on the Madeira job." His voice was low, but the threat was still there.

It was a waste of time. He could intimidate almost any man in London just by looking at him, but he had no idea how to handle women.

"Give most sods an office and a secretary," Gower said, "and they soon forget what it's like to work at street level. Well, I bloody haven't." He glared round at the dozen detective sergeants he had collected together in Interview Room B. "Fear," he continued, "that's the key. You keep the villains shit-scared of you, I'll keep you shit-scared of me, and we'll have a workable system."

There was no wonder they called him Toad behind his back, Scott thought. He looked like one: big, gleaming eyes, squat, powerful body – and poisonous. There were those who said that Chief Superintendent Ronald Gower was a good cop, and those who said he was a bad one. It depended on how you defined your terms. He was unquestionably financially honest – but his methods were sometimes dirty. He had a good arrest record – but it was not always the right man who got sent away. The two things everybody agreed on were that he was totally dedicated to his job – and that he was a right proper bastard.

"Don't think I don't know that your Chief Inspectors bitch about these meetings," Gower said. "Not correct procedure, is it? Well, the next time they start whinging, tell them from me that if they don't like it, all they have to do is get off their fat arses and start doing their jobs properly."

As Gower shuffled through the crime sheets, the sergeants sat in silence, each trying to make himself as inconspicuous as possible. The Chief Superintendent pulled one sheet out and smoothed it on the desk. The waiting men sank lower into their chairs. Gower's glassy eyes scoured the room, finally settling on a middle-aged sergeant with a perpetually worried look.

"These lorry hijackings, Sergeant Waters," Gower said. "What have you got?"

Waters cleared his throat. "We . . . er . . . believe it's Manchester Mike Swanson, sir," he said, "but we've nothing we can pin on him at the moment."

"Seven lorries in two months, and no arrest. It's a big black stain on your record," Gower snarled. "You'd better find something – and quick – unless you fancy ending your career as *Constable* Waters."

Gower's jaw suddenly clenched and his eyes seemed to burn with new fire. Scott knew what that expression meant. Talk of failure almost invariably brought his mind round to his own *bête noire*, the man he had pulled in five or six times and hadn't been able to hold, the man they knew was responsible for countless robberies but who had done time only once, before Gower was even posted to the Met. Scott sighed, and waited for the inevitable attack.

"Sergeant Scott," Gower rasped, "you're supposed to be our resident expert on the subject – what's Frank Mason up to these days?"

"Very quiet, sir," Scott said. "That job at the Midland Bank in Cheltenham last October had his MO all over it, but since then there hasn't been a whisper."

"How much did that job net?" Gower demanded.

"One hundred and thirty thousand, sir."

"One hundred and thirty thousand, six hundred and twenty-five," Gower corrected him. "Split four ways, and with Elsie's talent for spending, most of that must have gone by now. He'll be planning something new, and I want to know what it is. Top priority on this. Put pressure on your grasses, call in favours, let a few of the smaller fish off scot free if they come up with anything useful. It's three years to my retirement," he glared at all the seated sergeants, "and if I don't get Frank Mason by the time I pick up my gold watch, some bastard's going to suffer."

Five

Elsie looked out of the window at Hyde Park. It was only the beginning of November, but the stark, bare trees, shaking in a howling gale, made it seem like mid-winter. She was sick of England and its bloody weather, she yearned for a kinder climate, like the one in Madeira.

The thought of the Portuguese island took her mind back to her problem, and she frowned. Frank was acting very strangely these days. Sometimes he seemed elated; on other occasions he would be gloomy, as if weighed down by a heavy burden. But always, whatever his mood, there was the sense of purpose about him which she had first noticed in Madeira.

It wasn't a new woman – he was still knocking off that slag Linda. So, reluctant as she was to admit it, it was just possible that he was planning a job. It would fail, of course. It would be the most bungling amateurish raid in the whole history of bank robbery.

And maybe that wouldn't be a bad thing. With Frank out of the way for the next twenty years, her dad would have to keep her. And as long as she was discreet about it, she could have lots of other fellers on the side – younger fellers with a bit of class.

No, her pride wouldn't let her do it. Even though the robbery would fail, the very fact that it had happened at all, without her knowledge, would mean that Frank had pulled one over on her. And she was not about to give him that satisfaction.

She heard him moving around in the hallway, and by the time she got there he was already halfway into his camelhair coat.

"Bloody awful day to be going out," she said.

Mason shrugged the shoulders of his coat into position. "Just fancied a drink."

"I fancy one myself," Elsie said. "Mind if I come along?"

"If you like."

The pause was almost imperceptible, but Elsie, who knew him so well, noticed it. "On second thoughts," she said, patting her curls, "the wind'll ruin my hair-do. Frank, do you know how much money we've got left?"

"Not exactly."

The liar!

"About two hundred quid in the house, six thousand three hundred in the safety deposit box, and whatever you've got in your wallet."

And that was another thing. She'd never kept too close a track on money – when they ran out Frank could always rob another bank – but she was sure there should have been more than that. Frank might have been buying expensive presents for Linda, but that wouldn't account for it all. Whereas, if he was planning a job . . .

"As little as that," Mason said, but he didn't seem worried.

"It takes a while for me to set up a job, you know that," Elsie said. "And once it's fixed, we need seed money. It's about time I started thinking about the next one."

Early in their marriage, the mention of a new job had always excited him, but over the last couple of years it had instantly induced a depression, and for days he had walked round like a condemned man. Now, she watched as, apparently unconcerned, he slid on his gloves.

"You're right," he said, opening the door. "Put your mind to it." He stepped into the corridor. "And I'll keep a look-out for any likely prospects myself."

The door closed, and he was gone. Elsie stood still for almost a minute, scowling at herself in the mirror, then returned to the lounge.

The sky outside the window was hung with heavy grey clouds. It looked as if it might snow. Elsie picked up the phone and dialled a seven-digit number she knew off by heart.

"Hello? Yes, it's me," Her voice had lost its edge, and gained instead a syrupy, little-girlish quality. "No, I know I haven't . . . You know how it is, I've been busy . . . No, just things. But I have been missing you, Daddy, honestly I have." The syrup ran so thick that to anyone other than a doting parent, it would have been cloying. "Next week definitely . . . Listen, Daddy, there's something I want you to do for me . . ."

The gloves had been the easiest; as long as they were leather that was all that mattered, and he'd bought the first pair that fitted him in Harrods. There hadn't been much difficulty with the white suit either; he'd had it specially made and paid for it with the sweetener Mason had given him. It was when he had come to the shirts and ties that he'd run into problems – the shops simply didn't sell that sort of co-ordinated stuff any more. Still, he'd persevered, and it had paid off; the white shirt with discreet brown stripes and white tie with brown rectangular motif looked really sharp. Arnie felt as comfortable in the clothes as he did in the role model he had adopted to fit his position in the gang – Michael Caine in *The Italian Job*.

Not that it was an easy part to play, he told himself, as he sat on the dinky pink chair in the bed-sit. Not with the supporting cast he'd been given.

"You've done well, Arnie," Mason was saying. "A bloody good team."

A bloody good team. That was just what Arnie meant about the supporting cast – Noel Coward's Mr Bridger would never have used words like that.

"There's just one missing," Mason continued.

The married man who'd recently done bird. Arnie raised one gloved hand, the index finger pointing towards Mason, the others curled back into the palm. He'd been practising the gesture in front of the mirror, and knew it looked good.

"It's difficult, Mr Bri . . . Frank," he said. "I've only come up with one name, and he's not really suitable."

"Who?" Mason asked.

"Harry Snell."

"Solid feller, grey hair, got a wart on his nose?"

"That's him."

"How tall would you say he was?"

"About six foot," Arnie said, puzzled. How big did you need to be to wield a shotgun?

Mason smiled with satisfaction. "He'll do."

There'd been no weak link in *The Italian Job*, all the team had been real pros. Time for Michael Caine to step in and save the operation.

"You haven't seen him, Frank," Arnie argued. "He's just served eight of twelve and his nerve's gone. Even when he's talking to you, he can't sit still. He jumps every time a car backfires. Get him in a bank with a shooter in his hands, and Christ knows what will happen."

"Don't worry," Mason said, "he's just the sort of bloke I'm looking for." He turned to his lieutenant. "Right, Tony?"

"Right," Horton agreed.

The cameras were neatly laid out on the coffee table, and, one by one, Nigel was lovingly cleaning them. He never brought them out when Linda was at home because it always provoked an argument.

"You don't need all them," she'd say, "not for the kind of work you do. If you kept one and hocked the rest, we might have a bit of money for a change."

He gave into her on nearly everything, but he would never pawn his cameras. Now that he could no longer afford to sail, his skill as a photographer was the only thing he had left to take pride in.

He was in the middle of cleaning a lens when the doorbell rang. Jehovah's Witnesses or a debt collector! Nobody else ever called. He ignored it, and carried on with his task. The bell rang gain, more insistently this time. Nigel didn't even look up. Whoever it was would get bored eventually and go away.

The caller abandoned politeness and began hammering with his fist. Nigel laid the lens gently back on the table, then took his temper out on the door by flinging it open to reveal – Frank Mason. He backed away immediately.

"Hello, Nigel, old son," Mason said, smiling. "You took your time. You deaf or something?"

"I . . . no . . . I wa—"

"Mind if I come in?" Mason asked, but he had already stepped over the threshold.

Nigel had never been this close to Mason before. He realised for the first time that it was not the man's size that made him intimidating – he could give him an inch, certainly no more – it was his aura of hardness. He was sure that even if it were possible to sneak behind Mason and hit him with a sledge-hammer, the bastard would not go down – because he didn't want to.

Nigel looked wildly around the living room and saw it through Mason's eyes: the furniture, good when his father bought it, now outdated and battered; the carpet, visibly worn; the walls, with their faded, browning paper.

"Could do with a few quid spending on it," Mason said.

Nigel had to get away, if only for a minute. Had to have time to pull himself together without the overawing presence of Mason to distract him.

"Drinks," he said. "I'll get us some drinks," and fled to the kitchen.

He picked up two glasses to put on the tray, and they clinked in his trembling hands. He opened the door of the cupboard where he kept the booze – his father had had a private pub built in the cellar of his house – and surveyed the pitiful collection of bottles. A cheap supermarket gin, a British sherry, some Bulgarian wine. He uncapped the gin bottle and took a long swig. It was oily and unpleasantly fiery, but it gave him the courage to return to the living room.

Mason was sitting on the sofa, one of the precious cameras in his paw. Nigel wanted to kill him for even touching it, but instead he said, "We've got gin, Mr Mason, but we've just run out of tonic."

The seated man aimed the camera at him and clicked the shutter. Nigel felt a stab of pain in his chest.

"Doesn't matter about the drink, Nigel, old mate," Mason said. "I didn't come here for that."

He was holding out the camera in front of him. Nigel willed himself to step forward and take it from him, but his legs would not obey the command.

"Very nice equipment, this. Good with it, are you?"

"One of the best," Nigel said, and for once there was no wobble in his voice.

"That's what I'd heard."

Mason put the camera down on the battered coffee table, then reached over and patted the seat of the easy chair.

"Sit yourself down," he said.

As if this was his flat, and I was only a guest, Nigel thought – but he did as he'd been told.

"Linda mentioned that I've got a bit of work I might be able to put your way, didn't she?" Mason asked.

There was something about the way he said 'Linda' that told Nigel that this was her secret lover. He was burning with rage – but at the same time he was chilled with fear. "She's told me," he said.

"Well, it's more than a bit of work," Mason explained, "it's a major part of the operation, and one that calls for your particular talents." He pointed a finger menacingly. "You tell Linda any of this, and I'll break every bone in your body."

"You can trust me," Nigel said, and he thought to himself: You really *can* trust me, because I'm shit-scared of you.

Mason looked around the room again. "You don't want to go on living like this, Nigel," he said. "And you don't have to. You do this job for me, and I'll see you get the same cut as everybody else. Might even be enough to retire on."

If Mason had offered him a couple of hundred quid, or even a couple of thousand, he wouldn't have been worried.

He knew his own worth. But he was offering serious money – for Nigel's particular talents – and that scared him almost as much as the thought of what Mason would do if he turned him down.

"What's the job?" he asked.

Mason told him, quietly, confidently – but firmly. Then he left.

The second the door clicked behind him, Nigel rushed to the bathroom. He knelt over the toilet bowl, alternately gagging and puking. The bathroom tiles swirled before his eyes, but that was less disturbing than what was going round in his head: the job Mason had offered him – and he had promised to do; the scheme he had come up with to pay Mason back for taking Linda off him.

Working for Mason meant, at worst, a long time in prison. Working against him could mean ending up dead. He knew his plan was fraught with danger, but knew, too, that he was going to do it anyway. As a fresh batch of vomit rose in his gorge, he wished to God he'd never had the idea.

Mason needed the drink he'd told Elsie he'd gone out for. He stood against the bar of The Duke of Argyle and wondered why it was that so many pubs were named after dukes. No, he didn't, he corrected himself, he wondered if he'd got the timing right. Start things moving too early and word would get around; too late and the operation would fall irredeemably behind schedule. He'd had to recruit Portuguese Pedro when he did, just to make sure the silly little bugger stayed out of jail until Christmas. And he'd had to tell Nigel now, because Nigel would need to make arrangements. But he'd been taking a chance both times.

He turned to the plan as a whole. It was a thing of beauty, a delicate balance of forces – it was a hare-brained scheme full of 'What ifs?'. There were days when he felt sure he could pull it off. And there were days like this when all he wanted to do was run back to Elsie with his tail between his legs, begging her to go over The Plan to find its flaws – or, if she didn't like it at all, to come up with another one.

And why not? She had a few lines around her eyes, but her hair was still glowing blonde, and she had kept her figure – it was almost as good as Linda's. He didn't love her, that was true, but then he didn't really love Linda either. He wondered, if he really tried, whether he could to make his marriage work.

He saw the two heavies in the mirror behind the bar, the second they came through the door. They were both twenty-six or twenty-seven. One was about his height; the other was shorter, but made up for it with the breadth of his shoulders. They were hard; not like the kids in Spooner's Snooker Hall thought they were – but really hard. They walked up to the bar, and stood one each side of him. The barman came across and the taller one shook his head in a way that made him scuttle rapidly to the other side of the pub.

"There's a bloke wants to see you," the shorter one said.

"Is there?" Mason replied, sipping at his drink.

The shorter one grabbed his arm in an iron grip. "Now!" he insisted.

Mason put his glass down on the counter. "I should think you two could take me in the end," he said, "but I wouldn't half make a mess of you first."

"Let go of him," the taller one ordered. "Mr Sims doesn't want no trouble."

Mason had known all along who had sent them. These two would not have dared treat him like this unless they had really heavy backing. Still, he clicked his fingers, feigning surprise.

"Mr Sims? Of course, it's Son-in-law's Day. Has he got me a present? There was a lovely fluffy panda in the newsagent's window and . . ."

"Let's go," the taller one said.

No sense of humour, these fellers.

Mason looked around Sims' 'study'. It had changed for the better over the years; Persian carpets, antique mahogany desk – over which Sims probably perused his daily copy of the *Sun* – Regency furniture. Sims had become very rich since the day he moved into drugs and prostitution, the day Frank had decided to leave the firm and set upon his own.

A crucifix with a three-foot high Christ dominated the room. Mason marvelled at the anatomical accuracy of it; he could count all the ribs, even the veins in the feet were visible. The artist had caught the hanging man in a moment of exquisite agony, as he was twisting his body in a futile attempt to relieve the pain.

Sims had had people nailed up, Mason heard. He wondered if he'd used the crucifix as a model.

The oak-panelled door opened, and Sims entered the room. He was dressed in a three-piece tweed suit, and looked like a country gentleman up in town for the day. Until you saw his eyes. There was nothing of the jovial squire in them.

"If you needed to talk to me, I'm in the phone book," Mason said. "I don't like having nursemaids sent after me, Ted."

Sims laughed. "Don't take it to heart, Frank-boy. I just wanted to see you in a hurry. The lads may have been a bit over-keen, that's all. It's hard to get good help these days. Drink?"

"Whisky," Mason said. "Didn't have time to finish my last one."

Sims walked over to the bookcase filled from top to bottom with weighty tomes bound in Moroccan leather. He pressed Plato's *Republic* and the middle section slid up to reveal a cocktail bar. He mixed the drinks, and handed Mason his.

"I hear you're planning a new job," he said.

"Yeah?" Mason replied, noncommittally. "Where'd you hear that?"

Elsie! Bloody Elsie!

"Let's just say there's a whisper," Sims told him.

"It's news to me," Frank said. "Unless Elsie's got something up her sleeve."

Sims walked over to his desk, and sat on the edge. "The way I heard it," he said, "you were planning a job without Elsie. Cutting her out. And we all know what the next step is, don't we? I believe in the sanctity of the marriage vows, Frank. 'Till death us do part' – if you get my meaning."

"What's the going rate for rubbing out son-in-laws?" Mason asked. "Ten grand?"

"About that," Sims agreed, "if you want a proper job doing. But I don't have to pay, I've plenty of friends left in the business who'd do it for free, just as a favour."

It was probably true. Sims had retired, but you never really retired in his line. The two heavies waiting outside the door were proof enough of that. Mason considered the possibility that by nightfall he might have become a permanent resident of the River Thames.

"So," he said, "you got the whisper. Your first thought was, 'No, not Frank. He's been a good son-in-law. He helped me take my mob to the top. I'd never have got so big, I wouldn't have had all this,'" he gestured round the room,

" 'if it hadn't been for Frank.' That's what you thought, isn't it?"

"It might have been," Sims said.

"But then, because you're a suspicious old bastard, you said to yourself, 'But if Frank is planning a job, he'll be getting a team together.' So you got on the blower to see if you could come up with some names. Right?"

"Right," Sims replied. He seemed less certain now that Mason had taken the offensive.

"And what names did you come up with?"

Mason knew that he was managing to keep his face bland, but he could not control his fingers which were gripping, ever tighter, on the chunky whisky glass.

"Well," Sims said, "there was Tony Horton for a start."

"Oh, come on, Ted," Mason said, faking exasperation, "of course there'd be Tony. That doesn't prove a thing. It's like the Old Bill saying they know I've turned over a bank because I've got a tenner in my wallet."

"Harry Snell?"

"Don't know him well," Mason said. "Loser. Done bird two or three times. Still inside, isn't he?"

"Just come out."

"And when have I ever been bloody stupid enough to use somebody who's still punch-drunk? Anybody else?"

If Sims had come up with the wrong name, he was dead. He had to bank on the old man having uncovered the weak link in the chain. He raised his whisky glass to his lips, and waited.

"Well," Sims said reluctantly, "there was some talk about Portuguese Pedro."

Mason choked on his drink. For a full fifteen seconds he coughed and spluttered, then, with eyes filled with tears, he looked up at Sims. The old gangster seemed distinctly uncomfortable.

"Portug . . .uese Pedro!" he gasped. "Portuguese Pedro. Do you really think I'd have a wally like him working for me?"

Sims smiled, half-amused, half-embarrassed that he had even suggested it. "No, it don't seem likely, does it?"

"Mr Sims says we're to take you wherever you want to go," the shorter heavy said sulkily from the driver's seat.

"Take me back to my flat. You know where it is?"

"We know," the taller one said.

He bet they did. The bastards.

Mason looked out of the side window. A few delivery vans chugged along half-heartedly, stopping briefly to make a drop. The occasional pedestrian could be seen, huddled up against the cold, scurrying along the pavement. Sheets of newspaper were picked up by the wind, swirled through the air until it was tired of playing with them, then dumped, unceremoniously, against the nearest lamppost or dustbin. It was a filthy day, and the Edgware Road seemed the most depressing place on earth.

The two thugs in the front did not speak, either to each other or to their passenger, and Mason was glad of it. He needed time to think. It appeared to him as if his whole life had been dictated by circumstances beyond his control. Had he ever had any choice about drifting into petty criminality, and from there to the Ted Sims Mob? He did not feel as if he had.

The years had not brought greater freedom, they had only imposed heavier restrictions. Marriage to Elsie had never worked, could never work. He could never be his own man because there was always Ted Sims in the background.

He was not sure he could pull off the Madeiran job,

69

especially now, because if Ted could pick up the whispers, then the Law could, too. The whole thing might be over before it ever got started. But it was a chance he had to take – the only real chance to break free he'd ever had.

"Ooo, that's lovely, Bruce," Linda said. "Again, please, again."

Her head, inside the hood, felt pleasantly warm, and her toes prickled. This was her favourite time of the week. She popped another chocolate into her mouth and turned the page of her glossy magazine.

"Can I move on now, lovie?" Bruce asked. "I'm getting rather bored with this foot."

She looked down. She could only see the top of his head, his thick, brown, virile hair. "All right," she said, "but I might want you to go back to it later."

"Anything you say, duckie," Bruce lisped. "The customer's always right."

Most of the clients thought Bruce was gay, but she knew different. He wasn't just doing his job down there, he was taking every opportunity he could to look up her skirt. Sometimes when the massage and manicure was finished, he had such a hard-on that he could hardly walk straight.

Today, she was wearing black see-through panties with little pink butterflies on them. She opened her legs wider. She was feeling good herself, so why not give him a treat?

Nigel resented these visits to the beauty parlour. 'You don't need to have your hair done every week,' he was always saying, 'we can't afford it.' But somehow, knowing that he had to give up other things in order to scrape the money together so she could indulge herself only made it all seem more luxurious.

"So where are you going for your holidays, Bruce?" she asked.

70

"Wha . . . I . . . sorry, lovie, I was miles away."

Not miles, she thought, just a couple of feet away – at the top of my legs. The idea that she could have so much power over a man gave her a warm glow.

Her good mood was shattered by the thought of Frank. She didn't seem to have too much power over him these days. She could still have him panting and begging in the bedroom, but outside was a different matter. He used to tell her everything, all his problems, all his frustrations. Not that she had been particularly interested, but at least it had shown that she had a hold on him. Now, despite her having asked him several times, he had refused to tell her why he needed Nigel. And although she was part of the firm, she was sure that he was having meetings without her.

"How's that, sweetie?" Bruce asked. "Like it, do you?"

"Lovely," she said absently.

She wasn't sure that it would be a good idea to run off with Frank, even if he still wanted her to. Seeing him a couple of times a week was all right. But living with him? He certainly wouldn't let her get away with things like Nigel did. She'd have to become a one-man woman, and even with someone like Frank that could become boring after a while.

And there was another thing. You needed a lot of money to retire, and however big the bank haul was, there were too many people wanting their cut. If Frank would take more than his twenty per cent, say – in round figures – a hundred per cent . . . But she knew it was useless to try and persuade him.

What she needed was a new man, not a worm like Nigel, but someone a little more pliable than Mason – and rich! Now if she could find someone else in the gang a little less scrupulous about seeing that everybody got their fair share . . .

And once you put it like that, the choice was obvious.

Six

Portuguese Pedro pushed the door open, and looked around. Outside, the puddles were freezing over, but the saloon bar of The Crown, packed with Friday night punters, was almost oppressively hot.

No one noticed him standing there – but that would soon change. After he'd pulled the job with the Mason Mob, he would be a man to reckon with. In his imagination, Pedro played out the scene. A noisy pub a few weeks hence: the door swings open; the loud conversations stop almost immediately, and heads turn. 'It's Portuguese Pedro,' someone whispers, 'the man behind the big robbery.'

At the tables, the men smile ingratiatingly, hoping that he will favour them with his presence. He raises his left eyebrow and every woman in the room thinks, ecstatically, that the gesture was directed at her.

"Shut that bloody door, you stupid little bastard," a voice called out. "there's a bleeding gale blowing in."

Pedro walked quickly over to the bar and ordered a pint. When he came to pay, he produced the roll of tenners that Frank Mason had given him and nonchalantly peeled one off. He could see that the barman was impressed.

"Have one yourself," he said.

"That's very kind of you, sir. I'll have a Remy Martin."

The barman charged him for a brandy, but made no move to serve himself with one. Pedro looked around the crowded room for familiar faces. In one corner sat Fat Sid the bookie, a huge barrel of lard encased in a loud check suit. Next to him, wearing a donkey jacket with WIMPEY written across the back in large white letters, was Roadie O'Brien. There was so little of the third member of the company visible that he appeared to kneeling on the floor rather than sitting on a stool – Half Nelson.

"Small fries," Pedro thought to himself, "piggies-bank robbers."

But even so, he felt the need of company. He sidled over to them, and sat down uninvited.

Sid looked across at him. "Piss off, you Portuguese dickhead!" he said, without rancour. "We're talking business."

Pedro was offended. These jump-up shits didn't know who they were talking to. "I just thought I buy you fellers a drink," he said.

He pulled out his wad of tenners, and saw Roadie O'Brien's eyes light up. "Well, if you're buying, Pedro," the Irishman said, "I wouldn't mind one for the road."

"Me neither," squeaked Half Nelson.

Fat Sid frowned and stroked his treble chin thoughtfully. "All right, you little greaseball," he said, as though he was doing Pedro a favour. "I'll have a double whisky."

O'Brien had not specified which road they were having a drink for, and over the next two hours they toasted most of the British transport network. The three men continued their discussion of robberies past, present and future, noticing Pedro only when it was time to order another round.

The drunker the Portuguese got, the angrier he became.

These guys thought he was nothing, a loser. They didn't have no respect, they were just freeze-loading off him.

"So anyway," Fat Sid said, finishing off a story, "he had so much bother shifting these cans of Tesco corned beef that in the end he had to offer a free gift with every case."

"And what was it?" Roadie O'Brien asked.

"Half a dozen bottles of Californian bleeding syrup of figs."

Only Pedro did not share the general hilarity of the table. "Is small stuff," he said. "Chickens' feed."

"Small stuff?" Roadie said, almost choking with laughter. "Well, I suppose it would be – to Big-Time Pedro."

" 's right," Pedro slurred.

'Big-Time Pedro', he rather liked the sound of that.

"Anyway," Sid continued, "when he couldn't get rid of it even with the bleeding syrup of figs thrown in . . ."

" 's true," Pedro interrupted. "I'm working on a job right now."

"You're better than the telly, so you are," Roadie O'Brien said.

"I'm planning a job with Frank Mason," Pedro said, exasperatedly. "Me and Frankie going to pull a job."

"Frankie and Pedro," O'Brien said, giggling. "Crime's answer to Batman and Robin."

"You're not treating this seriously enough, Roadie," Fat Sid wheezed, taking a vivid check handkerchief out of his pocket to wipe his streaming eyes. "So tell me, Pedro, my old son, when's it going to be?"

'*I can't give any details yet,*' Frank had said, '*not even to you Pedro.*'

"Soon," Pedro said, half-heartedly.

"And where's it going to be, my little bandito? Bank of England? Harrods?"

"I don' kn . . . Is a secret."

"I don' kn . . . Is a secret," Sid repeated.

His chins wobbled like jelly on a sweet trolley and he buried his head in Roadie O'Brien's shoulder. The Irishman, almost purple in the face, slapped the other man heavily on the back.

"You guys are bloody bastards," Pedro said.

He rose gingerly to his feet and picked his way carefully between the swaying tables to the door. If he hadn't been so drunk and so angry, he would have noticed that while Sid and Roadie were still convulsed with laughter, Half Nelson merely looked thoughtful.

The fire was burning as well as could be expected with smokeless fuel, but it wasn't giving off that cheery glow that made you feel glad it was raining and windy outside.

"When this job's over," Mason thought, "I'll get myself a stone cottage somewhere bleak. One with a fireplace that burns logs, so you can warm your arse properly and roast chestnuts in the ashes."

"I had a talk with your dad the other day," he said.

Elsie, sitting on the sofa, looked up. "Oh yes," she said. "How is he? Haven't seen him for ages."

"He'd heard a whisper that I was planning a new job," Mason continued, watching her face closely.

"He'd heard that, had he?" Her expression didn't change. Elsie was good at not giving anything away.

"Matter of fact, I am planning a job – or at least I've got the idea for one."

"Where?"

"A branch of Barclays, right in the middle of Liverpool."

"How'd you find out about it?" Elsie demanded.

By making a quick trip to Liverpool the day before.

"Tony noticed it when he was up there last week, chasing some bird. He says it's a beauty. Historic building so that they can't mess up the frontage too much with security bars and things."

Elsie put down her drink and walked over to the bookcase. She scanned the shelves and pulled out an *A-Z* of Liverpool, *Pevsner* on Lancashire and a large-scale road map of the north of England. They were the tools of her trade, just as much as the sawn-off shotgun was Mason's.

She walked over to the desk, took out a pad and a pencil, and sat down. "What's the address?" she asked.

Mason told her. She looked up the bank in *Pevsner*'s index, then read the relevant section. "Show me exactly where it is in the *A-Z*," she said.

Mason pointed it out.

Elsie studied the map with intense concentration. Sometimes she muttered to herself, occasionally she made a note on her pad.

"One-way street system here . . . Find out about parking restrictions . . . How many traffic lights? . . . How are they weighted? . . . Police patrols – are they regular? . . . Do they have any coppers on foot?"

When she had exhausted the area around the bank, she turned to other pages, following the roads on from where they disappeared off the previous map.

"That's the nearest police station . . . that road leads down to the docks . . . long way round to the motorway, but with the traffic flow . . ."

Finally, she picked up the large-scale road map and traced the red lines out of the city and into Lancashire, Yorkshire

76

and Cheshire. The process seemed to go on for ever. While she worked, Mason sat in the corner, his copy of *Gordon's Wild Birds of Britain* on his lap. Normally, the book would transport him from the narrow world where sparrows and blackbirds stood shivering on the windowsill, begging for crumbs, to a place in which the air was tangy with peat and heather and real birds – solon geese and petrels – were masters of the sky, and of themselves. Now, he could manage little more than a desultory flicking through the pages.

Elsie and her father were not on to him yet, but they were not far from it. If she didn't swallow this Liverpool job . . .

It was over two hours before she finally, triumphantly, put down her pencil. "Yes," she said. "Yes, I think I'm definitely on to something here."

Mason did his best to hide his relief. "The place'll need casing."

"Oh, will it, Frank?" Elsie asked. "I would never have thought of that. Well, since you seem to have taken over the thinking, when do you suggest we do it?"

Mason bit back a comment. If it all worked out, he wouldn't have to put up with this shit much longer. "There's no need for you to come at all," he said. "At least, not at first. You just tell me what to look out for. I mean, casing's not the same as planning, is it? It's more your spadework, and I'm good at that."

A patronising smile spread across Elsie's face, and Mason realised he had never disliked her quite so much as he did now. Yet he should be grateful, because every smirk, every condescending comment, made it easier for him to do what he had to do.

"Spadework. That's true," she said. "You're very good at it. OK, you do the routine stuff and I'll go up there when a bit of brainwork's called for. When d'you think'd be a good time?"

He shrugged.

"Dunno. How about just before Christmas?"

"Just before Christmas? Why just before Christmas?" There was an edge of suspicion in her voice.

"You always told me that the best time to spot a weakness in the security is when they're busy," Mason said. "So I thought, with the Christmas rush . . . Maybe I'm wrong."

"No, you're not," Elsie said, and there was some warmth towards him in her smile this time. "I'm forgetting how much I've taught you. Christmas would be excellent."

"So I could go up on the nineteenth or twentieth, stay until Christmas Eve, and be back in time for my turkey and three veg."

"That's right, Frank," Elsie said.

If he'd had a tail, he thought, she would have expected him to wag it.

He was both pleased and vaguely disturbed. The conversation had gone as well as he could have hoped – or had it gone *too* well? He would have been happier if Elsie had put up just a little more resistance.

The window into the staff toilet of the video warehouse was so small that they hadn't bothered to connect it up to the main alarm system; so small that it even almost defeated Half Nelson, who spent fifteen minutes twisting and grunting before he was finally through.

Once inside, it was simply a matter of walking into the store, picking up a machine, going back to the toilet, and handing it through the window to Roadie O'Brien. Then, while Nelson went back to get another one, Roadie nipped up the alley with the first, and deposited it in the stolen laundry van. The operation took around a minute per machine.

As Portuguese Pedro had said when they'd met in the pub a couple of days earlier, this kind of job was strictly 'chickens' feed', but at least it paid the rent.

"Thirty," Roadie said, after about half an hour. "That'll do. There's no point in pushing our luck."

He disappeared into the darkness with the last machine.

Nelson stood on the toilet seat, and leant towards the window. Arms and head first, then twist and turn until the right shoulder was clear. His feet groped blindly backwards, searching for the sink and a few inches extra height. As he wriggled, he felt the basin start to come away from the wall. He got his left shoulder free at the same moment as the support behind him collapsed with a loud crash. His legs were left hanging in the air, and a cold jet of water shot up his trouser leg.

Shit! Where the bloody hell was Roadie?

He tried to get his feet back on the toilet seat, and if he had been just a little bit bigger, he would have made it.

Try something else.

He put his hands against the outside wall, and pushed. It hurt like hell, but it was working. His trunk began slowly to slide out. Until he came to his bloody hips! They wouldn't budge, no matter how hard he pushed. Exhausted by his effort, he took his hands away from the wall, and the upper half of his body jack-knifed.

There may be worse situations than hanging upside down with your nose almost touching the brickwork, while at the same time your legs are being soaked by broken water pipes – but Nelson could not remember ever being in one. It was a relief to hear footsteps approaching down the alley.

"For Christ's sake, Roadie," he whispered, "give me a pull, can't you?"

Two hands grasped him, one on each shoulder, but instead of pulling, they lifted. On his way back to the horizontal, Nelson noticed that though Roadie had been wearing a black nylon anorak minutes earlier, his rescuer's sleeves were serge – blue serge. He raised his head and found himself looking into a familiar face.

"Evening, Sergeant Roberts," he said.

"Evening, Halfie," Roberts replied amiably. "You're nicked, my son." He gently lowered Nelson back into the position in which he'd found him. "I'm just going to get the car," he said. "You won't run away, will you?"

"Could I have a cigarette, please, Sergeant Roberts?" Nelson asked.

"You don't want to start smoking, Halfie," Roberts said. "It'll stunt your growth."

"Very funny, Sergeant Roberts," Nelson said. It was not the first time he had heard the joke.

Roberts slid his packet of Silk Cut across the table. Nelson lit one and greedily sucked in the smoke.

"You know," the policeman continued, "I used to think they called you Half Nelson because of your size. But that's not the reason, is it? It's because," he paused to give his delivery greater effect, "if it's not nailed down, you'll half-inch it."

"Ha, ha," Nelson laughed obediently. That was not a new line to him either.

"So," Roberts continued conversationally, "What do you think you'll get this time. A five stretch? Eight? You are a habitual criminal, you know?" He shook his head sadly. "Eight years inside is a long time for a little feller like you."

Nelson licked his lips nervously. "I don't suppose . . . I mean . . . if I told you something useful, would you put in a word for me with the prosecuting brief?"

"You know me, Halfie," Roberts replied. "Always willing to oblige an old friend – as long as the old friend is willing to oblige me in return."

Nelson searched his mind, picking on titbits to feed to Roberts, rejecting them, and looking for better ones. "That lorry hijack in Clapham," he said at last. "I've heard it was Manchester Mike and Billy Trench."

"I've heard that too," Roberts said easily. "Got any proof?"

Nelson shook his head.

"Then it's not much use, is it?" Roberts asked. "Certainly not enough to make me bust a gut helping you."

"Frank Mason's planning another job."

"Is he?" said Roberts, looking interested now. "And where did you get that piece of information from?"

"Portuguese Pedro. He's working on it with him."

Roberts slapped the table. "Come on now, Halfie," he said. "You can't expect me to swallow that."

"It's true!" Nelson said. "Honest to God. I saw him in The Crown the other night. He had a fist full of tenners, two or three hundred quid at least."

"Surprising," Roberts agreed. "I'm amazed that little shit Pedro had any money at all. But it doesn't prove he's working with Mason."

"He told me himself," Nelson persisted. "He wouldn't have dared say it if he wasn't."

"But would he have dared say it if he *was*?" Roberts asked. "Still, that's better than all that crap about Manchester Jack. Half a brownie point. OK, what else have you got?"

"I'm just an honest businessman," Arthur Daley protested.

"Oh, are you, Daley? Are you indeed?" Sergeant Chisholm demanded.

Sergeant Scott grunted in disgust, and flicked over to Channel Four, only to find himself in the middle of a comedy sketch about a policeman who couldn't tell his arse from his elbow.

He switched off. Typical, he thought, that on his one night off everything on the box seemed to be taking the piss out of the police. Maybe Chief Superintendent Gower was right; maybe they'd never get the respect they deserved until they stopped pussyfooting about and showed what hard bastards they could really be. One thing was certain: if he wanted to get on in the next three years, then it was only Gower's rules that mattered.

The phone rang. He picked it up.

"Malcolm?" said the voice on the other end. "Andy Roberts here. Sorry to disturb you at home."

"Doesn't matter," Scott replied.

It didn't, not if it was about work. He was quite prepared to give his job all his time, on and off duty.

"I've just booked a little no-count called Half Nelson. You might like to come down here and see him. He seems to know something about your mate Frank Mason."

"Are you sure this little creep – whatsisname – Nelson, wasn't just feeding you a line?" Gower demanded.

"Pedro may not be working for Mason," Scott said carefully, "but I've just put Nelson through three hours

82

of interrogation, and there's no doubt in my mind that he believes he is."

It was the first time Scott had ever been in Gower's office. It was an easy place to find, the standard Force joke went; you go past the men looking vaguely worried, turn left at those showing quiet desperation and when you reach the ones who seem positively suicidal, you're there.

The office didn't stink exactly, but it bore the smell of almost full-time occupation. Yet there were no personal touches like there were in other offices – no pictures of wife and kids, no flowers, not even posters on the wall. Nothing, except for a group of photographs pinned to the notice board; and though it would be true to say that they were there for personal reasons, there was certainly no affection attached to them.

Gower strode over to the notice board now, and pointed to a black and white print.

"That's Mason when I first pulled him in, fifteen years ago," he said. His finger moved on. "This one was taken about the time of the Hampstead job in '83. This is the most recent one – last year."

There were twenty-five or thirty pictures, none of them official. "Study that face, sergeant," Gower said. "He may be a brute, but he's no fool. If he is using Portuguese Pedro, there's got to be a reason for it."

"How d'you mean, sir?"

"Pedro's a bleeding idiot," Gower said. "So if he's on the team, it must mean that the job calls for a bleeding idiot."

"Shall we pull Pedro in, sir?" Scott asked. "Put a bit ~~a~~ ~~bit~~ of pressure on him?"

Gower shook his head disgustedly. "You young coppers,"

he said. "Put the boot in first and think later, that's your motto."

"I'm sure he'd talk, sir."

"Well of course he'd bloody talk, he's nothing but a little wanker! But what would you learn? You'd find out about a job Frank had been planning, but which he'd have called off the second you collared Pedro."

"So what do we do, sir?"

"Better to wait till there's a raid with Mason's MO all over it. Then the little Portuguese turd'll know something worth pulling him in for. And sergeant, once you have got him inside you can be as rough as you like, and I'll be willing to swear under oath that I saw him fall down the steps on the way to the interrogation room."

He leant forward and examined another photograph of Mason, this one with Tony. The two men had their arms around each other's shoulders, and Mason was looking at Tony and smiling affectionately.

"Oh, you can smile, you bastard," Gower said, "but you won't make a fool of me for much longer."

He placed his thumb on the picture, so that the nail dissected Mason's face. He pressed harder, then slowly, deliberately, began to twist. When he removed his thumb again, there was only a hole where Mason's head had been.

When he turned round, his glassy eyes were bulging and his toad-like mouth had a venomous twist. Scott coughed discreetly, and watched as his superior slowly returned to normal.

"If we lived in a decent society, sergeant," Gower said, "one that had real respect for law and order, we'd have the manpower to keep Mason under twenty-four hour surveillance. As it is, since there's more bloody social workers than there are policemen, we'll have to settle for less. Put men on him whenever they're available."

"I'll watch him myself when I'm off-duty, sir," Scott said.

Gower grunted, as if that was already understood.

"I want regular reports," he said, "not through your DCI but straight to me." He flipped his address book, scribbled down a number on his pad and handed it to Scott. "I go on leave on the nineteenth of December. If anything breaks while I'm away, you can reach me there."

"I've already got your home number, sir."

"Aye, well, I won't be there, will I?" Gower said belligerently, "I'm going on holiday."

Gower on holiday? Gower getting away from it all? Scott found the idea so incredible that he let it show on his face.

"Find that surprising, do you, sergeant?" Gower asked.

His mouth, like an open wound, was set in a sarcastic smile.

"No, sir . . . I . . ."

"Health reasons. When you've been up to your neck in shit for as long as I have, some of it's bound to end up on your chest." He coughed, then spat a huge wodge of green phlegm into the wastepaper basket. "So that arsehole of a police doctor gave me two choices, didn't he? Get away to a warmer climate once every winter, or start thinking about early retirement. I trust you think I made the right decision."

"Yes, sir. Of course."

Scott felt hot under the collar. He glanced down at the number Gower had given him. A lot of digits – the old bastard wasn't going to Torquay, that was for sure.

"Spain, sir?" he asked.

"No," Gower replied. "A small island off Africa. Name of Madeira."

Seven

I t was freezing in the car, but there was no way of heating it without turning on the engine, and Nigel didn't dare do that. Besides, it was not only the cold that made him shiver – it was also the thought of what Mason would do if he found him there.

The first time, he had followed Linda on foot, dodging behind parked cars whenever she stopped to light a cigarette. And then she'd disappeared into the house in Matlock Road – she had her own key, the bitch! – and he'd been left in the street, feeling vulnerable and exposed. Now, it was easier. He could always tell when Linda was due to attend one of these meetings – there was an edginess about her that was a complete give-away – and he'd borrow a car and get here before her.

He heard footsteps and looked out of the window to see a ridiculous swaggering figure in high-heeled boots walking down the street. The Portuguese chap. With the ones already in the flat, that made four.

Mason and Tony Horton were at all the meetings Linda attended, but the composition of the rest of the group varied. He could recognise them all by sight now, though he could not put names to the faces. But then that didn't really matter, did it?

Someone else coming, the thickset man with grey hair. A jailbird, Nigel was sure of it. He could tell by the way he walked, short careful steps, as if he were afraid he would suddenly run out of pavement.

The man rang the bell. Nigel could not see who opened the door for him, only that the man seemed reluctant to go in.

Doesn't like enclosed spaces, Nigel thought to himself.

That was probably all of them. Now there was nothing to do but wait until they came out again, and he wondered whether tonight there was even any point in doing that. He looked down the street, assessing conditions. It was a filthy night, bitterly cold. The freezing fog swirled around the lampposts, trapping them, smothering them. He shivered, and an involuntary spasm ran the whole length of his body.

It was then that he saw the figure – a vague black shape standing perfectly still. He sat, mesmerised, for five long minutes, and in that time it never moved. It seemed to be watching, watching the house, just like he was. Then, suddenly, he realised with horror that it was not the green front door that had the spectre's attention, but the car – and him! As if it had read his thoughts, it began to drift slowly, inexorably, towards him. The closer it got, the clearer its shape. Yet at the same time it became blacker – more menacing.

I must go, he thought, his mind flooded with a torrent of panic. I must go.

He willed himself to turn the ignition key. But fear had locked his hands to the steering wheel. He sat, trembling, as the awful form got closer and closer. Then a gloved hand knocked commandingly on the window, and, moving like a zombie, he wound it down.

He had feared the figure would be a policeman – and now he saw who it actually was, he wished it had been.

It was to be the last meeting before the robbery. Pedro, sitting on the bed, looked around at the rest of the gang. Frankie, pinning a map on the artist's easel he had brought with him; Linda, lying on the bed, showing all that leg – dirty cow; Tony-Boy standing by the door; Harry Snell, almost burying the tiny pink chair he was sitting on.

Harry Snell. Harry Smell would be more like it – he had a stink of fear about him. Harry Smell. Yes, he liked that.

"Right," Frankie said, "let's get started. Up till now, only me and Tony have known all the details . . ."

But only for this job, Pedro thought. When Frankie find out what a good job I do, he make me his Number Two and Tony-Boy can go screw himself.

"Once you know the specifics, you'd better be very careful to keep your mouths shut. I'll personally cut the balls off anybody who repeats any part of this."

They all nodded their heads, Pedro a little guiltily. He wished he hadn't blabbed to Roadie, Sid and Halfie. But it didn't matter, he hadn't known nothing then, so he forgive himself.

Frankie told them the name of the bank, the day of the robbery, and how they were going to do it.

When he'd finished, he said, "Now we'll go through it again, just to make sure we've got it right. Those of us involved in the actual robbery will be travelling separately to the island, and when you get there, you're not to contact anybody else until the time agreed. Which is when, Harry?"

Harry Smell shifted uncomfortably. He didn't know! Pedro put his hand up.

"Yes, Pedro."

"The ones in the A Team meet at the car. The B Team meet them at the bank."

He said 'B Team' with special pride.

"Good," Frankie said. "Now are we sure we're clear on this?

Nobody sees anybody else until then. If you run into somebody accidentally, ignore them."

He handed out street maps.

"OK," he said, pointing to the one he had already pinned up, "the first two cars will be here, and here. Both places are well away from the centre, so there shouldn't be any danger of them being parked-in. The third car will be here, on Rua Castanheiro. The route it's to take is marked. Now I don't want you taking any of these maps with you. Right? You memorise the bloody things, and then you burn them. Now there's one more car, isn't there? Which one's that, Pedro?"

"Is the one I hire the day before, Frankie. I drive it roun' the route, two, maybe three times."

"Good. Now the shooters. Harry?"

This time Harry Smell knew the answer. "They'll all be in the same place, but we're to pick 'em up at different times."

"And do you know your own times?"

Everybody nodded.

Pedro wondered where Frankie was going to get the shotguns from. They couldn't take them on the plane, so they'd have to buy them in Madeira. There was some hunting on the island, but a foreigner asking to buy a shotgun – four shotguns – would be noticed. It didn't matter. Frankie was smart. Frankie think of everything.

"Now the most important thing is . . . not to get nicked," Mason said.

They all laughed.

"There are two safeguards against that already built into this job," he continued. He produced a cassette out of his pocket and slid it into the player on the dressing table. The motor whirred, and then a tinny voice, but still recognisable as Pedro's, said, '*Maos pra arriba* – Put up your hands'.

"Pedro's Patent Portuguese Course, there's a copy for each of us. Listen to it, memorise it. It's nothing complicated, just things like, 'Keep them covered', 'Pass me the bag', 'If he doesn't hand over the money, blow his bloody brains out'. You won't have to use any of it, but you'll have to be able to recognise it when you hear it. Why's that, Harry?"

"We want them to think that it's a Portuguese gang what's turned the bank over, so the only feller who'll be talking, giving orders, will be Pedro."

The only feller who'll be talking, giving orders, will be Pedro, the Portuguese repeated in his mind. Him!

"Now the fail-safe. It's just possible that the police'll work out it's an English gang, and then, of course, they're going to suspect us three right away. They'll come straight to our hotels and start asking questions. Linda, Susan and Mrs Snell will give us alibis – 'Where was your husband when the bank was being robbed?' 'Why, officer, he was in bed with me, just getting his leg over.' – but they won't believe 'em. We'll probably get taken down to the station. But they'll never be able to hold us – not without the money. And that's where Pedro comes in again."

The Portuguese felt his chest swell with pride.

It was still foggy and cold outside. Tony kept his head down as he walked along the street, so he did not notice her until he was almost at his car. She was leaning back against the bonnet, her legs widely spread.

"It's awful weather," Linda said, "so I thought you might give me a lift home."

They had spaced out their departures as usual, leaving five minutes between each one. Linda had been the first to go, he the next-to-last. That meant she had been wait-ing fifteen minutes on the frozen street for him to turn up. Why hadn't she waited for Frank? And what would Frank think when he came down the stairs in a couple of minutes?

"A lift?" she asked again.

"Yes . . . sure," he said quickly.

He got into the driver's seat and opened the passenger door. She seemed clumsy getting in, almost falling over on top of him. As she shuffled around, getting comfortable, her leg brushed his and he felt an electricity that was far from static.

At the corner of the street, he hesitated. "Which way do I turn?" he asked.

"That's up to you," she said, "but I would have thought that, as a gentleman, the least you could do would be to invite me back to your place for a drink."

Her hand fell, apparently accidentally, on to his thigh, but she made no effort to remove it. He could feel her long scarlet nails gently digging into his flesh. He cleared his throat, and turned left – homewards.

Linda looked around the living room of Tony's flat.

"Very nice," she said.

The tennis ball of indecision had been battering its way back and to across Tony's skull ever since Linda had first brushed against him.

— Frank was his boss, and Linda was Frank's mistress.

— But he really fancied her.

— Frank had been good to him, taught him all he knew.

— Just look at them boobs, straining to escape from her dress.

— Frank had always played straight with him.

91

— What he didn't know couldn't hurt him.

— But if Frank did find out? He'd chew him up into little pieces and spit him out again.

— How could he find out? It was as much in Linda's interest as in his to keep this quiet.

"Do I get that drink, then?" Linda asked.

"Oh, sorry! What do you want?"

Match suspended.

"Something long and cool," Linda said throatily. "Something that will take you a while to make."

Now that she was on the court, it was two against one. He did not see how his conscience – or even his fear – could resist the onslaught much longer.

He went into the kitchen and filled two highball glasses with crushed ice from the dispenser. When he returned to the living room, Linda had not moved.

"Well?" she asked.

He walked over to the drinks cabinet and pulled down the flap. As he reached for the vodka bottle, he saw that his hands were shaking.

"What are you making us?" asked the voice behind him.

"Harvey Wallbangers."

"Very appropriate!"

He poured the vodka over the ice, then added Galliano and orange juice. Behind him, he heard the sound of a zip being slowly, seductively, drawn down.

"Don't turn around," Linda ordered. "Look at the picture on the wall."

"It's not a picture," he said, "it's an engraved mirror. The *Cutty Sark*. It's an advert for the whisky, really."

Even as he spoke, he thought how absurd he sounded. He was angry with his himself. He must have had dozens – scores

– of women up to this flat, and none of them had affected him like this one did.

"Doesn't matter what it is," Linda said, amusement evident in her voice, "just look at it."

Obediently, he fixed his gaze on the clipper. Behind him, he could hear a gentle rustle, and knew that it was Linda's dress sliding to the ground. Stern, anchor, sails. Mainmast – tall, rigid. In the silvering that had survived the etcher's art, he could see small areas of pink flesh reflected.

"Right, you can look now," Linda said.

He turned . . . She was not completely naked – she had kept on her stockings and suspender belt. He ran his eyes hungrily up and down her body; her breasts, with brown protruding nipples, her slim waist, the mound of black pubic hair, the slender legs.

He realised that he had automatically picked up the drinks and was holding one in each hand. It made him feel helpless and slightly ridiculous. He made a move to put them down again.

"Stay exactly where you are!" Linda said.

She walked across the room, stopping when she was directly in front of him, her breasts almost brushing against him. He wanted to touch her, but he still had the bloody glasses in his hands. Linda took one from him.

"Let's take these through to the bedroom, shall we?" she suggested.

"That was great," Linda said. "You're really fantastic."

They had just made love in Tony's king-sized bed. Before that, they had made extensive use of the thick carpet and the armchair in the corner.

"Really fantastic," Linda repeated. "I mean it."

A complacent smile played on Tony's lips. He knew that a

lot of what she said was probably just flattery, but even so, he thought he'd been pretty good.

"You know," Linda continued, "Frank can be really stupid sometimes."

He wished she hadn't mentioned Frank. Even in the glow of post-coital well-being, it was enough to start guilt, like a chill, seeping through his body. And yet he knew that given the chance, he would betray Frank again . . . and again, and again. There was no way he could resist this woman.

She raised herself on to one elbow and looked into his eyes. "I mean, there's no need for him to divide the money up among all those people, is there?"

His mouth was dry, and there was a sudden pounding in his head. "Frank always plays straight," he croaked.

"Does that mean you have to as well? You're a big boy now. You've just shown that."

"We'd never get away with it," he said, because it was no use pretending that he didn't understand what she was saying. "Frank would kill us both."

"With all that money, we could go a long, long way. He'd never find us."

Names and faces swam before Tony's eyes. Jock McGuire, doing ten years in Durham; Wally Baxter, fourteen years on the Moor; Steve Hilton, twenty years, Isle of Wight maximum security. They were all about his age, but they'd be like Harry Snell when they came out, old before their time. His luck couldn't last for ever. Even Frank's luck couldn't. He was being offered the chance to make the break now, with a woman who was everything he'd ever fantasised about. And he could see exactly how it could be done. Given the nature of The Plan, it would be a doddle.

"No," he said. "I can't do it. Not to Frank."

Linda took his ear between her fingers, and nipped it with her nails. It was playful, but it still hurt.

"You're making me get nasty," she said reproachfully, "and I didn't want to get nasty, not with you. What d'you think Frank would do if I told him you'd raped me?"

"He wouldn't believe you," Tony said.

"Wouldn't he?" Linda took his ear between her thumb and forefinger. "Not even when I described that sweet little scar at the top of your thigh?"

It was morning. Outside, it was bitterly cold. Dogs taken for early morning walks seemed to resent the exercise, and even the shivering sparrows appeared to be coughing. The air was not much warmer in the kitchen of the dingy flat, where Nigel was slumped over the table, his head in his hands.

The door opened, and Linda entered the room. "What would you like for breakfast, Nigel sweetheart?" she asked.

He looked up accusingly at her. "You were out most of last night," he said.

Linda sat down opposite him, and took his hands in hers. "I was with Frank Mason," she said. "We've been having an affair."

Nigel lowered his head. "I know," he mumbled.

"No," Linda replied, her voice choked. "You don't understand at all. Don't ask me why it happened, because I can't tell you. Maybe it was because I was depressed by all this," she made an expansive gesture at the four walls which surrounded – almost imprisoned – them, "and when Frank offered me a bit of glamour I was too weak to resist. But we didn't make love last night, we only talked. He wanted me to run away with him, and I said I wouldn't, because when it came to it, I realised that it was you, not him that I loved."

Her eyes were full of tears. She walked round the table, sat on Nigel's knee, and buried her head in his shoulder.

"Don't speak," she said between sobs. "Just hold me. Make me feel safe. Make me feel protected."

He gripped on to her, and eventually the sobbing subsided and her body ceased to heave. She looked up at him, her eyes moist.

"I do love you, Nigel," she said, "And I want to be with you for ever. Only . . ."

"Only?"

"Only even though it's all over between Frank and me, I can't be sure that I won't get depressed again and be swept off my feet by the first rich man who comes along. That's the way I am. I'm not a very good person, Nigel, but I do try. Honestly."

He clasped her to him again, and rocked her gently. Her hand reached round and stroked his hair. For several minutes there was no sound but the ticking of the kitchen clock, then Linda said, "Nigel?"

"Yes," he answered sadly.

"If I could think of a way for us to make money, lots of money, so I'd never be tempted again, would you help me?"

He was not easy to persuade, but she cried again and told him that she loved him, and in the end he agreed.

"Thank you, sweetheart," she said. "Now if you don't mind, I think I'll go for a walk."

"Do you want me to come with you?" he asked.

"No. I want some time alone – to think about what a bitch I've been to you and see if there's a way that I can ever make up for it." She kissed him tenderly on the forehead. "I won't be long."

She did not walk far, only to the phone box round the corner.

"Tony?" she said, when her call was connected. "It's me. The stupid bastard fell for it."

Part Two

Line

Is it possible to succeed
without any act of betrayal?
Jean Renoir: *My Life and My Films.*

Eight

The snowflake fluttered down towards the ground. In a second or two, it would be re-united with its brothers and sisters to form a small part of the thin white carpet that was already covering the pavement. It was only a few feet from its destination when it was diverted by a faint air current and ended up crashing, like a kamikaze plane, into the nose of Chief Superintendent Gower.

Gower brushed it away angrily. Nineteenth of December and already it was bleeding snowing! That was what came of playing 'White Christmas' on the wireless all the bleeding time. Well, it could snow all it sodding-well liked once he'd taken off, but if those bureaucratic bastards at the airport dared to cancel his flight . . .

Blood pressure, Ron, he told himself.

He pushed his trolley into the terminal. Families stood guarding suitcases, long-haired yobs sat on their rucksacks. The place looked like a World War II re-settlement centre. Far too many people could afford package holidays these days – and half of 'em were probably paying with bent money, too.

He spotted his check-in desk at the same time as he noticed that a woman with three small kids and a trolley full of luggage was heading for it too. Bugger that! He

99

increased his speed, never taking his eyes off his rival for the next place in the queue. The woman had less distance to cover, but she was hampered by the slowness of her children. He was just going to make it.

His arm was jolted as metal clashed against metal. He looked up. The man pushing the offending trolley had short white hair, neatly combed, and wore heavy tortoiseshell glasses. Not as old as he might be taken for, Gower thought. Probably an old-fashioned accountant or a solicitor.

The woman with the kids had reached the back of the waiting line, and smiled at him triumphantly. He glared at the white-haired man.

"Why don't you look where you're bloody going?" he demanded

"It wasn't my fau—" the man began, in a confident, plummy voice. Then his mouth flapped wide open and the eyes behind the heavy glasses darted wildly back and forth. "Yes . . . sorry. Will you excuse me."

He disentangled his trolley and pushed it hurriedly away.

The woman was well ahead in the queue now, but Gower took some consolation from the fact that one of her children looked as if he was about to be sick. His mind returned to the white-haired man.

I know you, you bastard, he thought. I'm sure I do.

Only, the last time they had met, he hadn't been a solicitor or an accountant. He was a villain – the Chief Superintendent could smell them a mile away. But what the hell was his name?

His name, according to his passport, was Arthur Blake, and his profession was listed as chartered surveyor. But the passport was a fake, and the outwardly placid respectability was only skin deep. Beneath it lurked Alec Guinness's Smiley, nerves of steel, ready to penetrate enemy territory. And it was only by peeling off several more skins, until you had virtually no onion left at all, that you would eventually reach Arnie the Actor.

At least, that had been the case until five minutes earlier when Gower had bumped into him and he had first recognised the Chief Superintendent and then seen, with horror, that his luggage was tagged for Madeira. Now it was definitely Arnie who was standing in the Skybar, knocking back double whiskies at a rate which impressed even the barman-who-had-seen-it-all.

As Arnie, increasingly fuzzily, saw it, he had three choices. He could go home and forget the whole thing. He could ring Mason now, tell him what had happened, and thereby pass the buck. Or he could go ahead as planned. Disadvantages of Option A? He wouldn't get paid – and Mason would probably kill him. Option B? If Mason called the operation off, he would lose the money just as surely as if he'd chickened out himself.

Which left Option C. Gower might or might not have recognised him, but, apart from the fake passport, he had done nothing wrong. And he would be well away from the island by the time the robbery took place. With Gower there, the odds were on Mason getting caught, in which case he still wouldn't get his money, but there was a slim possibility that Mason could pull it off, and some chance of getting his bread was better than no chance at all. He had made his decision. He felt it was one of which George Smiley would have been proud.

"Now remember, Frank," Elsie said, "don't book in at—"

"Don't book in at an expensive hotel," Mason interrupted,

imitating her voice. "Stay at some commercial place where they won't pay much attention to you. And for God's sake, when you're in the hotel, try to act like a rep."

It was stupid of him to antagonise her at this stage.

"Sorry, Elsie," he said. "You know I always get edgy during the planning."

Elsie smiled. "That's all right. It's nice to see you're learning."

He looked at his watch. Arnie should already be in the air on his direct flight to Madeira; Tony and Susan would be flying there via Lisbon the next day; Nigel had left for Brighton more than a week before; Pedro's train was careering through central France; Harry and his wife . . .

Don't think about it, he told himself. Not when Elsie's watching you. "Time to go," he said aloud. "I'll ring for a cab."

"No need for that," Elsie said. "I'll drive you down to the station."

Why the bloody hell was she being so helpful now? "I don't want to put you to any trouble," he said.

"It's no trouble at all."

Against all odds, Elsie managed to find a parking space near Euston and was still with him when he entered the station. He had left some leeway for getting to his flight, but he had never anticipated this. He resisted the temptation to look at his watch again.

He bought his ticket, and Elsie walked him to the gate. "Now remember everything I've taught you, Frank," she said, "and you'll have no trouble in Liverpool."

The idea seemed to amuse her. It had been a long time since he had seen her amused.

He got off the train at Reading and caught the first one back to London. At Euston, he took a taxi to Paddington Station where he handed in his suitcase of clothes suitable for the north in winter at the left luggage and redeemed the case he had deposited the day before. This case was new, and so were the clothes inside it – he wasn't going to run the risk of Elsie going through his wardrobe and wondering where his summer shirts had gone.

He was worried about the time, and that made him a little careless. But even had he been at his sharpest, he probably wouldn't have noticed the man who had been following him ever since he left his flat, and who was now standing by W.H. Smith's bookshop, watching the case swap. He wouldn't have noticed because the man was highly trained, and very, very good at his job.

It was her first flight, the elderly woman sitting next to Gower had explained, and she was terrified. She'd sworn they'd never get her up in an aeroplane, but her best friend, who lived on Madeira, had just lost her husband, and she felt it was important to get to her as quickly as possible, didn't he agree? Poor Madge, she and Leslie had been so looking forward to their retirement, they'd only been there for four months and this had to happen . . . She'd been so wrapped up in her story and her nervousness that it had taken her some time to realise that Gower, far from being sympathetic, was being deliberately rude. Now she sat with as much of her back to him as the seating permitted, maintaining an offended and dignified silence.

Gower's own mood improved the closer they got to their destination. The old bag had really pissed him off with her inane chatter, but the landing in Madeira would give him his revenge.

"Terrible cross currents here," he said, conversationally, when the seat-belt sign came on. "Blows out from between the mountains, you know. They tell me the pilots crap themselves every time they have to do this run."

The old woman sniffed disdainfully, but tightened her grip on the armrest.

"Then there's the airstrip," he continued. "It's one of the shortest in the world. That's why they've got to slam on the brakes as soon as they land."

The woman's lips were thin and trembling.

"They don't always make it. A few years ago one overshot the runway and went arse over tip into the sea. Pity you were yattering at me while the stewardess was showing us the life-jacket drill, isn't it?" Gower said, twisting the knife in the wound.

The wheels bumped on to the tarmac, the reversed engines roared, the plane juddered, slowed and finally came to a halt almost at the edge of the runway. The seat-belt light went off, but Gower's travelling companion seemed reluctant to move. He squeezed past her, bullied his way up the aisle past passengers who were struggling with baggage in the overhead lockers, and descended the steps on to the tarmac.

The air was mild. A gentle breeze was blowing from the west, carrying with it the smell of the sea and the vegetation. Less than a hundred yards away, the terminal building was ablaze with light and activity. Gower started to walk towards it.

He was right behind the solicitor-accountant as they went through the green customs channel. There was something wrong with the man's walk. It wasn't just that he was drunk, though he'd obviously had a skinful. It didn't look natural, it didn't look real, it looked – copied. That was it! He was bloody acting!

"Have you read the regulations, senhor?" a customs official asked the white-haired man.

"Yes."

"And you have nothing to declare?"

"No."

The official patted the counter. "Would you mind to put your suitcase up here and open it," he said.

The fake solicitor-accountant looked confused. "I . . . well, I might have . . . I mean I . . ."

"Just open your suitcase, senhor," the customs man said, tonelessly.

Gower moved on, out into the airport lobby. The voice, too! He was sure he recognised the voice!

Even out of uniform, the man waiting for him – pot-bellied, hook-nosed, his thick black moustache drooping at the ends – looked like a comic South American dictator. They shook hands. There was no outward display of warmth in the greeting, and yet, if there was anyone in the whole world Gower could call a friend, it was Inspector José Silva of the Policia Judicial.

It was a strange relationship, Gower thought, as Silva loaded his cases into the boot of the Peugeot 206. Since they had first met at an international police conference, Gower had visited Madeira four times, and on each occasion Silva had spent most of his free time with him. Night after night they would sit on Silva's balcony, a bottle of whisky between them, looking down on the lights of Funchal. They said very little, but were perfectly relaxed and happy together. Yet Gower couldn't honestly say that they liked each other.

Perhaps they found a bond in their common experiences. Both were without women; it was nearly thirty years since Gower's wife had run off with the milkman, and Silva had been a widower for almost as long. But it was not a sense of loss that they shared, rather it was the absence of such a sense. Gower suspected that Silva, like himself, had very little interest in sex; but the subject was one of the many things they did not talk about.

They set off along the narrow, twisting coastal road that led to Funchal. Silva, like most Madeirans, drove with a casual ease which bordered on recklessness, apparently oblivious to the fact that there was a sheer rock face on one side, and a drop down to the sea on the other.

Maybe the real basis of their friendship rested – as most friendships did – on self-interest, Gower pondered. Silva liked to be associated with a big-city policeman, and Gower himself got a feeling of superiority from this parochial cop's silent respect. Or perhaps they stuck together like lepers, because no one else was comfortable having them around.

That's the whole bloody trouble with holidays, he thought angrily. They give you too much bastard time to think.

He wished he were back in London, giving some really hard-case criminal a working over.

"The regulations clearly state one bottle of spirits, senhor," the customs official said. "You want to pay me one thousand escudos or you want me to take the whisky?"

Arnie wondered which would create less comment – paying or not paying. He was regretting his Smiley decision, made under the influence, because now that he had sobered up somewhat he realised there was a much bigger charge than holding a fake passport which they could get him on

– conspiracy. Conspiracy to commit a robbery. Conspiracy to commit a murder, if Frank's gang wasted anybody!

"You pay or I take it?"

"I'll pay."

He handed over the money and waited while the officer wrote out a receipt.

Arnie walked towards the courtesy bus for the Casino Park Hotel. His hair was dyed white, he was wearing glasses, he told himself. He was in disguise. If Gower had penetrated that disguise, he'd have said something immediately. Given the sort of copper he was, he'd probably have arrested him at Heathrow, even if it had meant missing his holiday. So, at worst, Gower had suspicions, and as long as he could keep out of the bastard's way until the job was done, they'd never grow into anything else. But if he did see him again, something just might click in the Chief Superintendent's brain.

He stopped some distance from the bus. If Gower was on it, he'd take the next flight out, whatever the consequences when Mason finally caught up with him. There were a dozen people waiting impatiently to be taken to the Casino Park – three couples, a family with children and two old ladies. Of the toad-like policeman there was no sign. It was going to be all right. Confidence restored, he headed for the bus.

The road down the hill was decorated with hanging lights arranged in elaborate patterns, the trees in the park were festooned with countless coloured bulbs. Funchal was dressed up for Christmas.

Silva drove along the front, past the old ship which had once been one of the island's vital links with the mainland, and which now, in its new incarnation, was a fashionable bar. Young men in short-sleeved shirts walked hand-in-hand with girls in brightly coloured dresses; older couples sat at pavement cafés, sipping wine and watching the sea. Gower found himself making a mental review of his caseload.

As they passed the marina – masts bobbing gently up and down, rigging fluttering in the breeze – Silva turned to him.

"You didn't say which hotel you chose this time."

Every year, Silva suggested that Gower should stay with him, Gower demurred, Silva insisted, until finally, to their mutual relief, it was agreed that maybe next year Gower would be Silva's houseguest. Nor did Gower stay at the same hotel two years running. The atmosphere that existed between him and the staff after his two-week stay was usually sufficient to ensure that, whilst they would accept a future booking from him, he would not be welcomed.

Gower told Silva where to go and the Inspector whistled.

"You have treated yourself well this year," he said. "Five star!"

Well, why not? What else did he have to spend his money on?

They took the Avenida do Infante, passing the Parque de Santa Caterina, as brightly lit with decorations as the rest of the town. At the top of the hill, by the casino, Silva indicated left, and turned into the driveway of the Casino Park Hotel.

The girl standing at the British Airways check-in at Gatwick looked up to see not a ticket, but a police warrant card, held under her nose.

"Get yourself relieved for the next five minutes," Sergeant Scott said. "We need to talk."

Behind him, waiting passengers complained loudly. Well, as Gower would say, sod them!

Relief was soon supplied and Scott led the girl away to a quieter part of the terminal. "That man and woman who just checked in," he said, "what name were they using?"

"Mason. Why? Isn't it their real name?"

"Yes," Scott answered, surprised. "Well, his anyway. Where were they going?"

"Spain."

Scott felt a pang of disappointment. He had thought he was on to something when he'd started following Frank that afternoon, especially after the tricky train change at Reading. But now it looked as if Mason was merely giving his missus the slip and nipping off for a dirty weekend.

"Alicante, I suppose," he said glumly.

"No, Madrid."

Now, why the hell should Frank want to go to Madrid? Especially if he was taking Linda, who was strictly one of the bare boobs on the beach brigade if he was any judge.

Except . . . Spain was right next to Portugal, Frank was supposed to be setting up a job with Portuguese Pedro, Madrid had an international airport. It was all fitting neatly together.

He looked at his watch. The flight was due to take off in half an hour, another two and a half hours in the air, thirty more minutes while they collected their baggage and cleared passport control – if he put a call through to Madrid now, there could be a discreet reception committee waiting for Frank when he arrived.

Nine

There were two of them standing at the barrier outside Customs and Excise, one in a fawn overcoat, the other wearing a leather jacket. Their expressions showed neither the expectation of people waiting for relatives already four hours late, nor the couldn't-care-less attitude of couriers who, holding up their cardboard signs, feel they have already done enough. Instead, there was only deep concentration as they tried to match up the description they had been given with one of the emerging passengers.

"Give me a fag," Mason said to Linda.

"I thought you'd given up."

"Just do it."

She shrugged and flipped open her packet of Benson and Hedges. Mason took one and concealed it in the palm of his hand.

"Hang on," Linda said, fumbling in her handbag, "I've got my lighter somewhere."

But Mason was already walking towards the two men at the barrier. "Got a light?" he asked the one in the overcoat.

"*No hablamos inglés, señor,*" the policeman said.

We don't speak English.

The other man, already reaching into the pocket of

110

his leather jacket, looked shamefaced and let his hand drop back.

No worked-out common cover. Beginners!

Mason produced the cigarette and mimed a light. If the situation hadn't been so serious, it would have been comical to see the look of mock-realisation on their faces.

"Thanks," Mason said, smiling at them as he sucked on the cigarette, then he turned and walked back to Linda.

Shit, shit, shit!

He thought it had to be the Ford Mondeo, but on the motorway, in the darkness, he couldn't be sure. Even when it was still on the taxi's tail as they drove along the Calle de Alcala, it could have been no more than coincidence.

"Drive around," Mason told the cabbie.

"*Qué?*"

"Drive around." He made a circling motion with one finger then held up two together. "Small streets."

"Not railway station?"

"Not railway station," Mason agreed.

"Why are we doing this?" Linda demanded.

"Just a precaution, darlin'. I always take precautions."

The cabbie drove up the Gran Via and then signalled right. They were plunged into a maze of side streets full of early morning cafés serving grumpy, half-asleep workmen with coffees and cognacs. The cabbie twisted and turned the wheel, hooting his horn at pedestrians forced to walk in the street because so many cars had been parked on the pavement.

It was a slow, intricate journey and when, after passing the Infantas Cinema three times, the Mondeo was still behind them, Mason took the train tickets for the Lusitania

o+1

Express to Lisbon out of his pocket and slowly, deliberately, tore them up.

"Well I don't understand what all this is about," Linda said loudly, tucking into her fried breakfast with relish. "Why have we booked into this hotel for three days when the flight from Lisbon's—"

"The day before Christmas, darlin', I know," Mason replied, equally loudly. "So we don't have to leave here until the twenty-third." He lowered his voice to almost a whisper. "That's right. Why don't you tell everybody what we're bloody doing."

"There's no need to swear," Linda said huffily, but quieter. "I only want to know what's going on."

"I'll tell you as soon as I know myself," Mason said.

He looked out of the window across the Gran Via. The Mondeo was parked illegally on the other side of the street, Fawn-overcoat leaning casually against it. There was no sign of Leather-jacket, he'd be somewhere near the hotel entrance.

It *was* a low-level operation, Mason was sure of that now. The English police didn't know anything, they just had suspicions, and the Spaniards were keeping him under surveillance, a simple matter of professional courtesy. That was why there was only one car and the two tails were novices. But they were causing him as much trouble as if they'd been the most experienced men in the Spanish police force. He could lose them – easily – but then the low-level operation would be stepped up. Airport and railway police would be informed, car-hire firms would be checked on. Yet if he didn't lose them, then they would find out exactly where he was going – and that would be fatal.

112

He glanced at his watch. Seven o'clock. The plane out of Lisbon left at ten o'clock that night – just fifteen hours. And if he didn't catch it, there would be no Madeiran job.

'I've told you, Frank,' Elsie's voice echoed mockingly in his head, 'you should always leave the planning to me.'

There had to be a way out of the mess!

He forked a piece of egg into his mouth. It tasted of ashes. He pushed his plate to one side.

"I'm going up to the room to freshen up," Linda said.

"Don't be more than half an hour," Mason instructed her.

Not a long time to devise a scheme that would fool the Spanish police force with all its resources, but he daren't allow longer. Lisbon was only 700 kilometres away, but if he didn't come up with something soon, it might as well be a million. He bought a guidebook and map at reception and sat down to study them.

By the time Linda returned, he had a plan. It was not a thing of beauty, it was a desperate improvisation depending on the opposition acting exactly as he had predicted they would, and, more worryingly, on his getting a lucky break. It was inflexible, it was clumsy – but it was all he had.

"So what do we do now?" Linda asked.

"You," Mason replied, "have got a lot of shopping to do."

He handed her a fistful of money and told her what it was he wanted her to buy. They left the hotel together, then separated, Linda going left down a side street towards the Puerta del Sol, Mason heading for the Gran Via Metro station. At the entrance to the Metro, he bent down to tie his shoelace and risked a quick glance behind him. Fawn-overcoat, only a few yards away, suddenly became absorbed in a bookshop window; Leather-jacket, on the other side of the street, had stopped to light a cigarette.

Thank Christ they had both decided to follow him!

At the ticket office, he asked for a map of the system.

"*Plano?*" the ticket clerk asked.

Mason nodded, and was handed a small blue leaflet. He followed the signs to the southbound platform. There were perhaps fifteen or twenty people waiting; out of the corner of his eye he could see Leather-jacket.

A train rattled into the station. Mason got on, and stood just inside the doorway. He unfolded his map and pretended to study it. The whistle blew. Mason frowned as if he had made a mistake, and stepped on to the platform just as the doors were closing. He caught sight of Leather-jacket trapped in the moving train. He did not look around for Fawn-overcoat, but he knew he must be somewhere on the platform. Even amateurs like these did not make that kind of mistake.

He took the northbound train, changing at Alonso Martinez. He made no effort to throw off his tail. The longer they thought they had lost him accidentally, the more time he would have – and every minute was precious. He got off the train at Goya, and instead of walking to the exit followed the tunnel that led directly to the Corte Ingles department store.

It was only a little after ten o'clock, but already the place was crowded with pre-Christmas shoppers. Fawn-overcoat would not be more than fifteen yards behind him, which gave him only seconds if he wanted to make his break unnoticed.

He emerged in the bargain basement and took the escalator up. He behaved sedately until he reached the ground floor, then ran up the next escalator, pushing his way past the bag-laden shoppers. On the fifth floor, he headed for the service stairs and took them three at a time. He left by the side door and hailed a passing taxi. His heart was pounding and he was out of breath, but he had probably lost his tail.

"Malasaña," he told the cabbie.

Had he been in London, Mason would have known exactly where to look, but in Madrid, he could only guess. And the guess had to be right, because there would be no second chances – every minute that ticked away made it less likely he would catch his plane to Funchal.

At night, the guidebook said, the Plaza de Dos de Mayo was crowded with tourists and students who had come to listen to the guitarists and watch the acrobats and magicians. At a quarter to eleven in the morning the only people around were a street sweeper and a man walking his dog.

There was no time to go anywhere else. Mason began to walk up the steep street that led out of the Plaza. He was looking for anyone vaguely bent – a con man, a pickpocket, a mugger – but someone with two vital qualifications. It turned out to be a drug-pusher, making his first sell of the day.

He was in an alley, slowly and carefully counting out the bills in his hand while his pathetic client twitched and fretted. Both were so intent on the transaction that they did not notice Mason until he was almost on them, and by then it was too late. He grabbed them, one in each powerful hand, and slammed them against the wall.

They were both wearing anoraks and jeans. The pusher

was twenty-three or twenty-four, the customer younger. They looked up at him in wide-eyed terror.

"*Policía?*" the pusher asked.

"No, I'm not the police."

Mason could feel the young man relax a little under his grip.

"S – señor," he stuttered, "I am not a criminal. I sell only a little to pay for my studies."

He spoke English. One of the two hurdles out of the way.

"Can you drive?"

The pusher looked puzzled. "Yes," he said.

"How long have you had a licence?"

"Three years."

Mason turned to the buyer. "Have you got a syringe on you?"

"*Qué?*"

"Ask him," he ordered the pusher.

"*Tienes jeringuilla?*"

"*Sí.*"

"Tell him to give it to you."

The instruction was conveyed and the boy put a grubby hand in his pocket, produced the syringe, and handed it sideways to the pusher.

Mason took his hand off the customer's shoulder.

"Get out of here!'

The boy did not understand the words but he caught the meaning and scuttled off down the alley. Mason took a handkerchief out of his pocket and handed it to the pusher.

"Wipe the syringe!' he ordered.

The pusher obeyed.

116

"Now, hold it in your hand, carefully, so that we get some really nice fingerprints."

Reluctantly, the pusher did as he was told.

"Wrap it in the handkerchief – carefully so you don't smudge the prints."

When the operation was completed, Mason put the syringe in his pocket. "I want you to do a job for me," he said. "If you don't do it properly, I'll see the police get this. But that will be the least of your problems, sunshine, because I'll come back looking for you – or else send some of my friends, which could be even nastier. Understand?"

The pusher nodded.

"That's the bad side. The good side is that if you do the job properly, there'll be money in it – lots of money – some now, some later."

Mason read a mixture of emotions on his face – reassurance because now he realised that the man he was dealing with was not straight; greed at the prospect of the money; and a deepening fear as he came to realise that Mason was way out of his league.

He would do – he would have to do.

Although he could not understand the words, Mason could tell from the tone of the clerk's voice that he regarded the young pusher with grave suspicion. It was not really surprising; with his scruffy anorak and long, greasy hair, he did not look at all like the sort of person who usually deals with Avis.

"For how many days do you wish the car, señor?" his own Avis assistant asked him.

"Just the one."

"And are you paying in *metálico* – cash?"

"Yes."

"In that case I must charge you for the kilometres now. Any you have not used will be re-paid when you give in the car."

By the time this job's over, Mason thought wryly, the car-hire companies will have made nearly as much out of it as I will. "Fine," he said aloud.

He risked a glance at the other desk. The pusher was just signing the forms.

At the bar a group of lorry drivers was talking loudly, in the corner by the door the one-armed bandit was playing its punter-enticing tune, and the wall-mounted television was blaring out the early afternoon news. It was the third roadside cafeteria that Mason had stopped at, and by far the noisiest. But it had one big advantage over the others – the public phone was on a meter, so there would be no continual feeding in of coins to tip off those at the other end that he was calling long distance. He dialled the hotel.

"This is Mr Mason. Room Three-One-Seven," he said.

"Just a moment, señor," the clerk replied.

There was a faint click. A second phone being picked up. Someone – probably Fawn-coat or Leather-jacket – did not want to miss this particular conversation.

"What can I do for you, Mr Mason?" the clerk asked.

"Has Linda – my wife – come back yet?"

"Your room key is still in the *casilla*, señor."

"I see. Has she rung? Has she left a message?"

"No, señor."

"The bitch!" Mason exploded. "She's done it again!"

"Señor?"

"She's picked up another man. She's always doing it."

"Señor . . ." The clerk's voice sounded embarrassed.

"I'll find the cow," Mason shouted. "I'll find her if it takes me all day and all night. The lousy bitch."

He slammed down the phone, paid for the call, and left. Linda was waiting for him in the car.

"What's all this about?" she demanded.

"I told you – precautions."

"Well, I think it's crazy. I had to leave some nice clothes in that hotel."

"I gave you the money to buy some more this morning, didn't I?"

"Yes," Linda conceded, "but I liked the ones I left behind as well."

And that was Linda all over, he thought. Some wasn't enough for her – she had to have it all.

They made good time on the Spanish side of the border, travelling along a well-surfaced *autovía* by majestic mountains. Once they had crossed into Portugal, it was another story. Though the traffic was lighter, the roads were narrower. And to make matters worse, there appeared to be an extensive repair and improvement programme in place, so that every few kilometres they were brought to a halt by heavy-plant or single-file traffic.

Each time he was forced to stop to let a flock of sheep cross the road, each time he found himself stuck behind a slow-moving lorry, Mason edgily checked his watch. If they missed the plane, there would be no chance of booking another one – not that close to Christmas. And without him on the island, there could be no Madeiran job.

Once they hit the ring road which ran around Lisbon, they picked up speed again, but it was still going to be a push. Mason's original plan had been to muddy the trail a little, by parking the car somewhere in the city and catching a cab out to the airport. Now, he realised, he would have to run the risks entailed by leaving it in the airport car park.

He shook his head doubtfully. The Madeiran job had not even really started yet, and already it seemed to be coming apart at the seams.

Ten

G ower only just made it down to breakfast on the morning of the twenty-first, which was better than the day before, when he hadn't woken up until eleven. It was a sign, he supposed, that even if his mind didn't need the rest, his body did.

The previous evening, three quarters down the bottle of whisky, José had quoted him the island's annual crime figures – 67 crimes against order and public tranquillity, 36 against persons, 58 against property – as if he'd actually been pleased with them.

"Any murders?" Gower had asked.

"We did have one last year, but it was only a – domesticated? – one, and the killer give himself up."

How the hell would they cope with a proper crimewave? Statistics like that wouldn't last Gower's division a day. All right, his job could be frustrating, especially when the Commissioner of Police was an old woman who wanted criminals treated with kid gloves. And it was a strain, too: his blood pressure was too high, he smoked so much his lungs looked like kippers, and once in a while he'd experience a violent contraction of the chest muscles. But at least it kept him busy, gave him a purpose in life. He wondered what José used to fill his mind.

He spotted the solicitor-accountant sitting a few tables down from him. "I do know him," he said softly. "I definitely know the bastard."

He closed his eyes and tried to conjure up the scene. He could see a table in an interrogation room, with the other man sitting nervously across from him. His hair hadn't been white then, it had been brown – and brushed back, as if he thought he was Clint Eastwood.

What had he done? Robbery with violence? Housebreaking? No, he wasn't the type. Embezzlement or fraud would be more in his line.

Try the name then. Reginald something? Archie? Not quite right.

He had dealt with so many bad 'uns over the years that it was difficult, without the help of records, to pull out a name immediately. But it would come to him . . . it would come to him.

When he opened his eyes again, the other man had gone.

"It's time," Linda said. "If we don't go now, we'll be late."

Mason rose reluctantly from his chair. After what had happened in Spain, he didn't want to show himself outside the Madeira Savoy. But it was necessary – it was all part of The Plan.

They walked along the sea front to the iron kiosk where Mason had first had the idea – where everything had seemed so simple. A fair-haired young man in a Benetton sports shirt and light trousers was talking to a pretty blonde girl in a black and white dress. Mason was glad that Tony had bought Susan some new clothes.

'*Nobody sees anybody else*,' he'd said at the last meeting

Pedro attended. '*If you run into someone accidentally, ignore them.*'

But Pedro wasn't on Madeira yet, he wouldn't be arriving until the evening. Mason sat down. "Good flight?"

Tony merely shrugged.

Nothing was as it should be, Mason thought. Those last couple of weeks in London, Tony had been acting very strangely. After seven years of working together, of being friends rather than just associates, Tony had suddenly erected a barrier between them, as if he had something to hide.

"You seem edgy," Linda said. "Like last night."

Ah yes, last night. He had wondered how long it would take her to bring that up. The crossing into Portugal had stretched his nerves almost to breaking point, and when they'd finally arrived in Madeira, when they were finally in bed, he hadn't been able to get interested in sex, despite all Linda's encouragement. And she'd taken it as a personal insult.

That was all she saw in a man, he thought, a body to give her pleasure, a wallet to feed her acquisitive appetite. His dreams, his interests, meant nothing.

"I said, you seem edgy," Linda repeated, her voice grating on his mind like a nail dragged down a blackboard.

"Oh, piss off!" he snapped.

"Right!" Linda said. "Right, I will."

She stood up and flounced off down the street. Heads turned to look at her. A mistake, Mason realised. She shouldn't be making herself conspicuous – not yet. And they couldn't afford disunity on an operation like this one. He knew he should get up and go after her, but he couldn't bring himself to do it, not at that moment.

"Catch her up, Tony," he said. "She'll listen to you."

Horton looked startled. "Me? Why . . . Sure thing, Frank."

Linda was already fifty yards away, carving a path through the afternoon strollers. Tony jogged along the promenade after her.

"You shouldn't have spoken to her like that, Mr Mason," Susan said.

Had it not been for the obvious concern in her voice, he would have told her that he knew he shouldn't, but what the hell had it got to do with her. Instead, he just said, "You're right, darlin'."

His hands were on the table, clasped together in a tight knot of frustration, anger and worry. She placed her own on top of them. Her fingers felt cool and reassuring.

"You need to relax, Mr Mason," she said. "Try breathing deeply. That's what I always got Mam to do when she was in pain."

He did it to humour her. As he breathed in and out she stroked his hard knuckles, matching her rhythm to his. To his amazement he found that it was having an effect, that he was starting to feel better.

"You're a very nice girl, Susan," he said, smiling.

She smiled back at him. "I like you too," she said.

"That will be fifteen thousand escudos' deposit," the fresh-faced youth at Avis said, "and we will deliver the car to your hotel by ten o'clock tomorrow morning."

Nobody was keeping to the script, Arnie thought. If Gower had been at breakfast the previous morning, he could have ad-libbed. But Gower hadn't been, and he'd relaxed. Then, like the ghost of Hamlet's father coming on one scene too late, he had appeared that morning, and

Arnie, unprepared, had panicked and practically run out of the dining room.

And now this eager young man was saying that the car would be delivered to the Casino Park. Suppose the other two companies he still had to hire vehicles from insisted on the same thing. Three delivery men, three cars, all outside the hotel at the same time. How could he explain to them why he needed them all on the same day?

It was worse than just having a bad script, Arnie decided. It was like knowing that however well you played your part, the slating reviews were already set up in typeface.

"I'll pick it up from here," he said.

"It will be a pleasure to deliver it to your hotel, senhor," the youth said – and Arnie could have strangled him. "We are Avis. We try harder. And it may be a great disconvenience for you to come here. You see, although we say that you can have the car at nine thirty, that is only true if the last customer bring it back on time, and many of them, alas, do not."

"I'll risk it," Arnie said.

"And sometimes the car is very dirty and we have to clean it well before we can hire it to you. So you may, perhaps, be waiting here for an hour. You would be much more comfortable at your hotel – and there is no extra charge for delivery."

How would Smiley have handled this one? Even the complexity and intrigue in the world of international espionage seemed simple in comparison to booking a car through harder-trying Avis.

"It's a surprise for my wife," Arnie said desperately. "I don't want her to know I've hired a car until I'm actually in it. It's a . . . well, a surprise."

"Then we will park it by the side of the hotel and she will not see it until—"

"No," Arnie said. "I'll pick it up here."

The smile disappeared from the boy's face. "Very well, senhor," he said coldly. "If that is what you wish."

Arnie's lines were more polished by the time he booked the other cars – one from Hertz, one from Tower – and he received no more than mildly raised eyebrows for his eccentricity.

It would all come out after the robbery, of course, and the police would be on the lookout for an Arthur Blake, who needed three cars in one day. But by then Arnie the Actor hoped to be back in the Smoke, away from all the trouble.

Mason lay on his hotel bed staring at the ceiling. Ceilings would become a familiar sight if the job went wrong. He closed his eyes and tried to imagine what it would be like to be locked in a room hour after hour, to walk in a high-walled yard where there were no trees, no flowers, no birds. Could he possibly endure that kind of existence? For the next twenty years? No, he knew he couldn't. If they caught him this time, he would kill himself.

It's just nerves, he thought. It's always like this just before I pull a job.

But it wasn't. Because normally the plan was not so intricate. Because normally there were not so many things that could go wrong.

Yesterday had been the twentieth, today was the twenty-first. The job was planned for the twenty-third, and there was no way he could advance it, even if he wanted to. By now, the Spanish police would have realised that he was not returning to his hotel and would have begun to institute checks. He had covered his tracks as well as he could, but they would not be fooled for ever. First they would find out about the car – if only he'd had time to ditch it at somewhere other than the airport! – then about the plane. If they discovered he was in Madeira before the twenty-third, all the planning would be wasted. Worse than that, Elsie would notice that their last few thousand had disappeared from the safety deposit box – and tell her father.

Mason felt as if there were a pair of steel hands around his throat, their pressure slowly increasing, squeezing the life out of him. If only they would let just enough air get through to enable him to survive the next two days.

Eleven

It was just before a quarter to nine in the morning on the 22nd December. The man in the business-suit walked with the swagger of one who has achieved relative eminence at a fairly early age. Outside the bank he stopped, looked up and down the street, and then inserted several keys in the door. He entered the bank, closing the door behind him.

He have the keys to the door, Pedro – sitting in a parked car – said to himself, but he don' know how to open the safe.

He was thinking in English, because now he was a real London gangster.

Over the next fifteen minutes, several other staff arrived and were admitted, but it was not until five to nine that the older man turned up.

This is the manager, Pedro thought. He know how to get into the box.

At exactly nine o'clock, the blind on the door was raised and a disembodied hand flipped the plastic sign to announce that the bank was open.

Pedro waited for four minutes – 'That's all we have,' Frankie had said, 'four minutes' – then drove along the street and turned into a side road. He parked, timed another thirty seconds, and moved off again. It was important to simulate

128

actual conditions, Frankie had said. Pedro rolled the words around in his mouth: "Simulate actual conditions!"

Traffic was light in the town – Frankie had said that too, what a mind Frankie had! – and Pedro was soon on the road to the mountains.

It was six kilometres out of Funchal, where the steep climb had begun in earnest, that he got his shock. By the side of the road, in the middle of nowhere, was a wooden hut, and next to it was a long wooden pole on a metal swivel.

A roads block?

Pedro drove past it slowly and, when he was sure there was no one around, backed up again to take a closer look. A notice on the side of the hut announced that it belonged to the Policia Florestal – the Forest Police. The round metal sign on the pole contained the single word, 'Stop!'

It *was* a roads block!

His immediate reaction was to turn around and drive back to Funchal, find Mason and tell him all about it. But Frankie had said there was to be no contact under any circumstances. "Is an emergency," he told himself.

He calmed down a little. The road was not closed today, the twenty-second, there was no reason why it should be closed on the twenty-third. He was 'simulating actual conditions' and the actual condition was that the roadblock was unmanned. Besides, the Policia Florestal were not real police.

"Tree police," Pedro said to himself. "Pretty flower police."

They would not stop a desperate gangster like him.

He took the turn-off to the Pico do Arieiro, keeping his speed down to sixty kilometres an hour.

'Drive carefully,' Frankie had said. 'You've plenty of time and we don't want any accidents.'

Mist was rising from the fields and through it could be seen the vague shapes of sleepy sheep, nibbling lethargically at the grass. The cafeteria, where the road came to an end, was still closed.

'The tour buses don't start to arrive until ten,' Frankie had said. 'By then you'll have got rid of the money, and can drive back to Funchal just like any other sightseer.'

He was so bloody clever, that Frankie.

Pedro parked the car and stood looking at the trail that hugged the mountainside, sometimes sweeping sharply down, sometimes disappearing into the clouds. He climbed down the roughly hewn steps into the dip, counting them as he went. Thirty, fifty, seventy, ninety.

At the bottom, he began to climb again. Thirty, bastards-forty, bloody-bastards-fifty. He realised that city life had made him soft; that this walk, which would have meant nothing to him when he lived in the village, was making his calves ache. Sodding-bloody-bastards-seventy.

But he did not really mind the pain. Frankie could have chosen Tony-Boy or Harry Smell to hide the money, and instead he had chosen him – Big-Time Pedro.

"Is a great honour," he said to himself.

He turned the corner. Behind him, he heard the roar of a car engine, the staff of the cafeteria arriving for work, but turning round he found that he could not see the building itself. And that meant that the people there could not see him.

Beautisful!

He walked on another hundred metres and found what he

was looking for, a deep fissure in the rock, just off the trail. He bent over it, tried to reach the bottom with his hand, and found that he could not.

Perfect!

He collected a number of smaller rocks and strewed them innocently around near the fissure for use the next day. Satisfied with his work, he walked back to the car park, picked up his vehicle, and drove back to Funchal as just an ordinary sightseer.

With three car firms to choose from, Arnie put his money on Hertz – and lost. The car was not there at ten, was not ready until ten thirty, and by the time he had parked it at the pre-arranged spot and got back to Avis, it was already eleven.

"Good morning, senhor," said the clerk disapprovingly, glancing at his watch as he did so.

Hell hath no fury like a helpful young man scorned.

"Good morning," Arnie said. "Is my car ready?"

"It is ready since ten, senhor." He looked out of the window. "Soon, the mountains will be full of cloud, and you will have lost your view. Your wife will be very disappointed." He paused, before delivering his final coup. "And because you said you would pick up the car at ten o'clock, we must charge you from ten o'clock, even though you have not used the car."

"Doesn't matter," Arnie said.

He still had one more car to collect – at Tower – and the later he got there, the more suspicious they were likely to be.

The Avis clerk frowned. "What hotel did you say you were staying at, senhor?"

"It's in your records. The Casino Park."

"Please be so kind as to wait here."

"I'm in a hurry," Arnie said.

"You did not seem to be in a hurry earlier, senhor," the clerk replied. "But I will not keep you long."

He disappeared into the back room.

He's calling the hotel, Arnie thought. He could picture the lobby in his mind, and Gower, just handing in his key as the call came through. He wouldn't understand any of the conversation, but his ears would prick up when he heard Arnie's assumed name.

'Isn't that the white-haired man I've seen in the dining room?' he'd ask, as soon as the receptionist had put the phone down.

'Yes, senhor.'

'No trouble, I hope.'

'No, it was just a car-hire firm, making sure that he is a resident of this hotel.'

Gower would look at his watch. 'Hiring a car now,' he'd say to himself. 'Unusual that . . . unless he's hiring several cars at the same time.'

Paranoid, Arnie thought. I'm getting paranoid.

The Chief Superintendent probably didn't even know his assumed name. But still, it was hard not to be paranoid. Ever since he had first seen Gower, his tough Smiley shell had been cracking, and any second now it would shatter completely, leaving the fluffy, yellow, little Arnie completely unprotected.

The clerk returned. "I will fill out the documents now, senhor," he said.

His one break of the day came at Tower. The girl behind the counter was much more interested in polishing her nails than she was in his late arrival, and the documentation was completed with a minimum of fuss. By midday, the third car was in place.

He had only two more tasks to complete, then he would be free of the island – free of Gower. He turned down the hill and headed for the sea front.

"Mason's on the move, sir," Scott said over the long-distance line. "He flew into Madrid the day before yesterday."

Gower felt a quick stabbing in his chest. Why did he have to be away when Frank was pulling something?

"I want him watched twenty-four hours a day," he said. "Get the top brass to put pressure on the dagoes."

"They've already lost him, sir," Scott said.

"They've what?" The stabbing pain had settled into a tight, crushing band around his diaphragm.

"There were two men following him. He lost one on the underground and the other in a big department store. They seem to think it was unintentional. You know, he wasn't trying to throw them off, didn't even know they were there – it just happened."

Stupid bloody wogs! "It didn't just sodding happen," Gower snapped, "not with our Frank. So what did they do then?"

"The hotel got a call from Mason. He said he suspected Linda of having a bit on the side and he'd look for her all night if he had to. Anyway, they went up to his room, and all his clothes were still there, so they just sat back and waited."

"Jesus Christ!" Gower said.

If he had useless dickheads like that working for him, he wouldn't even trust them with directing the bastard traffic.

"When he didn't turn up in the morning, they ran a

check on airports and car-hire firms. Drew a blank with the airports, but it seems that Mason hired a car the day before and handed it in yesterday morning in Barcelona. So that's where the Spanish police are concentrating their efforts now."

Even through the pain, which was now throbbing as well as pressing, Gower thought he saw it all. There was a good reason for using a wally like Pedro. Mason was planning to pull a job in Portugal. And they were asking him to believe that Frank had driven as far from the Portuguese border as it was possible to get and still be in Spain.

"Did the description of the man who handed in the car match Mason's?" he demanded.

"They didn't actually see him, sir. When the office is closed, customers just park the car on the forecourt and drop the key through the letterbox. They're expecting him to turn up – they owe him quite a big refund – but he hasn't yet. When he does, the car firm have instructions to stall him and phone the police."

"He won't bloody turn up," Gower said, "because he isn't in bloody Barcelona. He didn't drive that car – my guess is, Linda did. Get 'em to check the car firm again, see if he hired a second car, and if he did, alert the Portuguese police and tell 'em to look out for it."

Frank would never have done a bunk from Madrid if he wasn't going to pull a job soon. Gower wondered how long it would take, if the need arose, to get a flight to the Portuguese mainland.

Arnie walked along the levada cut out of the hillside between Funchal to Amparo, a large canvas bag under his arm. Madeira has 2,150 kilometres of levadas – concrete water courses which start at high altitudes where the rainfall is heaviest, and flow, gently sloping downwards, all over the island. It is quite a remarkable number of irrigation channels for such a small place, but even if Arnie had known this, he would not have been impressed. The view of the town, the sea and the mountains, was breathtaking, but Arnie didn't care about that either. He was no longer George Smiley, operating with cool assurance behind enemy lines. Now he was Hardy Kruger – The One Who Got Away.

On either side of the levada were small banana plantations, nothing more than the backyards to numerous tiny houses. He reached a bend where the levada started to slope downhill. This was the place. The ground to his left was four or five feet lower than the water channel, so he jumped down. At the base of the nearest banana tree, he placed the canvas bag, then collected a few leaves that were lying on the ground and spread them over it. He looked at his work with satisfaction. The bag was invisible to the casual passer-by, but could easily be found by somebody who was looking for it. He checked his watch. It was time to get out. He did not want to meet the person who was due to collect the bag.

Pedro arrived ten minutes after Arnie had left. He glanced over his shoulder to make sure that there was no one in sight, then dropped off the concrete walkway into the banana plantation. He knelt down beside the bag and his hand went longingly to the zip.

'I don't want any of you opening your bags until you get back to your hotels,' Frankie had said.

The temptation was too great. He pulled on the zipper and revealed the treasures inside – black over-trousers, a black sweater, a ski-mask and the keys to a rental car. But best of all, there was a sawn-off shotgun. Pedro took

135

it out of the bag. Its barrel gleamed in the sunlight, its stock felt firm in his hands. He pointed it at the nearest banana tree.

"I am the B Team," he announced. "Put your bloodys hands up."

'No shooting,' Frankie had said, 'not unless it's absolutely necessary – and then only over their heads.'

But supposing there was no choice? Supposing the only way to escape was to shoot it out with the police? Frankie couldn't be angry with him for that.

He could see people pointing at him back in London. 'There goes Pedro Gomes. He killed two policemen in Madeira. You don't tangle with that bastard.'

It would be wonderful to be given the chance. As he placed the shotgun reverently back in the bag, he wondered once more how Mason had managed to procure the guns. He was a clever sod, Frankie.

"Arnold Hebden," Gower said loudly, startling the pre-dinner drinkers at the other tables. "Arnie the Actor."

His mind had not been on the white-haired man at all, he had been thinking of Frank Mason, but his subconscious, ticking away on its own, had come up with the name. Now what the bloody hell was Arnie the Actor doing on Madeira?

It was always possible he was on holiday, Gower supposed. Until the Government had enough guts to stop villains ever leaving the country, you would always get scum like Arnie frittering away their ill-gotten gains in the sunshine. But did people like Arnie ever really take a holiday? The world was full of mugs, especially in places like this, and Gower had never known a con man yet who could resist the opportunity if it was staring him in the face.

He left his drink and strode up to the reception desk.

The immaculately dressed young man on duty favoured him with a polite, helpful smile. Gower scowled back at him and was just reaching for his warrant card when he remembered where he was. His face creased into what he imagined was a good-natured grin.

"I've just seen a man I might know," he explained, "but I'm not sure, so I'm a bit embarrassed about approaching him." Tact? he thought to himself. Bloody subtlety? They wouldn't recognise me back in London.

"Perhaps you could describe this man, senhor," the clerk said.

Gower did, with the precise, clinical accuracy that was a product of nearly forty years of police work.

"Yes, that is Mr Blake."

Gower clicked his fingers. "So it is old Blakey. I thought it must have been." He feigned concern. "I hope I haven't missed him. Not after all this time. He hasn't checked out, has he?"

Acting? Bleeding Oscar-winners weren't in it.

The clerk consulted his register. "No, senhor," he said. "He will be here for another week. Shall I tell him you have been enquiring after him?"

If Arnie wasn't running a con, he wouldn't be using an alias. "No," Gower said. "Don't do that. I'd rather like to surprise him."

He went up to his room and called Inspector Silva.

"Is the man dangerous?" José asked, sounding worried.

For a second, the thought of Frank Mason flicked across Gower's mind. Two London villains on Portuguese territory at the same time was the sort of coincidence that Gower instinctively distrusted. But Frank would never be stupid

137

enough to pull a job on an island – where he would have no chance to make a getaway.

"All criminals are dangerous," he said, then conceded, "but Arnie probably less than most. Still, if I were you, I'd have him picked up immediately. You can hold him for using a fake passport until you can invent something a bit more serious. Listen, José, if you need any help in interrogating him, I'm available. You might learn something about British police methods."

He realised that for the first time since the start of his holiday he was sounding enthusiastic – and that his clenched right fist was beating a slow tattoo on the palm of his left hand. Of the pain he had been experiencing earlier in the day, there was no sign.

The *maitre d'* at Jardim's Restaurant glanced with grave distaste at the party in the corner. As the evening had progressed, they had drunk more and more and become louder and louder. People at the other tables had turned to look at them until the dark-haired woman – the one dressed almost like a prostitute with her plunging neckline and split skirt – had made some loud comment that sounded like 'rubber-necks'. Now the other diners were self-consciously intent on their food and, if they had to move their heads, made a determined effort not to look at the corner table.

It was the pretty fair-haired girl who the *maitre d'* felt sorry for. She seemed to have no place amongst this group of rough people. Not only that, she looked lost, as if the others were playing a game and had not explained the rules to her.

" . . .come on, Linda," the young man in the smooth suit said at the top of his voice, "you have to admit you're a bit like a second-hand dartboard."

The *maitre d'* did not understand the statement, but its tone told him all he wanted to know. He would ask them to leave immediately. They had run up a large bill, but the reputation of the restaurant was more important than a few thousand escudos.

Before he could make a move, the tart was on her feet, leaning across the table.

"Say that again, Tony," she shrieked. "Say that again."

The man laughed uneasily. "Well . . . I mean . . . you have had more pricks in you than—".

He got no further. The woman's hand flew through the air, catching his face with a crack that echoed across the whole restaurant.

Two wine bottles, knocked off the table, gurgled their contents on to the carpet, but apart from that there was total silence. Then the man came out of shock.

"You bitch!" he shouted. "No woman does that to me!"

He started to rise, tilting the table and causing plates and glasses to spill on to the floor. He was not quick enough; a tall dark man was already on his feet and forcing him back into his chair. Another couple took the tart by the arms and began to hustle her towards the door.

"Come on, Linda," the woman said. "Calm down. Let's get you home."

"I'm all right now, Mrs Snell," the tart replied. She turned to the man. "Tell her I'm all right now, Harry."

"You're all right," the man said, reassuringly, "but I think we'd better get you home anyway. Don't you?"

The tart nodded, and allowed them to lead her away.

The *maitre d'* was almost at the table when the big dark man blocked his way. He felt the man's hand on his shoulder and found himself being steered away from the disaster. It was a new experience to be shepherded through his own restaurant but there was something about the dark man . . . By the time he had abandoned the idea of trying to puzzle it out, they were already at the kitchen.

The man took out his wallet and produced his Visa card. The *maitre d'* looked at it dubiously and then, suddenly, the sense of superiority that came from being the captain of his ship, the lord of his castle, deserted him.

This man frightened him. Let him pay with his card, let him not pay at all, just as long as he left the restaurant. He looked up, apprehensively, to see if he had caused offence. But the other man didn't appear to be offended at all.

"You don't want the card, right? Fair enough." He put his hand in his pocket again and withdrew a plastic wallet of traveller's cheques and his passport. "You just tot up the bill and the damages. And listen, include a big tip for the waiters – they're good lads."

"Yes . . ." the *maitre d'* said uncertainly. "Yes, Mr . . ." he glanced at the passport, " . . .Mr Mason."

Twelve

The car, a Renault Megane, was parked just where Frankie had said it would be. Crouching down on the blind side, Pedro slipped on his black jumper and over-trousers. He was starting to look like a bank robber. But it was the mask that would make the real difference — studying himself in the mirror the previous evening, he had been amazed at the transformation. The slit eyes, the gashes for nostrils and mouth, created a face that was no longer recognisably his, a face that was evil and commanding. With the mask and the gun, he was a man to be feared.

It was three minutes to nine as he drew level with the bank. The blind was down, the plastic notice still turned to 'closed'. There was no sign of the other car.

'If it's not there,' Frankie had said, 'drive around the block.'

There was little traffic and very few pedestrians. Pedro passed the grey-haired manager a hundred metres from the bank.

"You got a bloodys shock coming," he mouthed at the walking man. "Oh, yes."

By the time he had completed his circuit, the other car, a black Volkswagen Golf, was parked in front of the bank. Pedro pulled in behind it, being careful not to get too close.

'We don't want to get parked-in,' Frankie had said, 'so leave a gap. Give Tony space to reverse.'

He thought of everything, that Frankie.

He looked at his watch again. Thirty seconds to nine. By five past nine it would all be over – it had *better* be all over.

'It's likely we'll be spotted when we enter the bank,' Frankie had said, 'but that still gives us four minutes.'

It didn't seem an awfully long time to Pedro, who had seen how quickly cops reacted on TV.

'The feller spots us, right?' Mason had explained. 'At first, he thinks he's seeing things, because he's just an ordinary bloke, and ordinary blokes don't get involved in bank robberies. Then he hesitates – what should he do? Call the police, of course. He's got to get to the phone box and put the call through. There's a delay while he's connected with the right department, especially in Madeira, where there's never been a bank robbery before. The cop on the other end can't believe it either, and it takes a while to convince him it's not a hoax. Add on his reaction time and travelling time, and we've got four minutes. But not a second more!'

At nine o'clock precisely, the plastic sign was turned. Pedro did not move. He was waiting for the signal. The Golf's brake lights flashed three times. That was it! Pedro reached for his ski-mask and pulled it over his head. He picked up his shotgun, opened the car door and ran towards the bank.

A little way down the street he could see two men, frozen to the spot. He pointed his shotgun at them, and they dived for cover. The power, the power!

Frankie, Tony-Boy and Harry Smell were in the bank,

black menacing figures, their shooters covering the eight startled bank employees.

"Maos pra arriba!" Pedro ordered, but the clerks, in the standard clichéd manner, already held their arms high in the air.

Pedro walked up to the manager and laid his gun lightly against his chest. The man almost fainted with fear.

"Take out the keys to the safe," Pedro said. "I want you to move very slowly. If you press the alarm, or we even think you are going to press it, we will kill you." He turned to the tall robber nearest the counter. "While I am with the manager, watch these bastards," he instructed, carefully using the exact Portuguese words that the others had learned from the cassette. "If anyone tries to be clever, shoot him."

And Frankie nodded. Frankie Mason was obeying his orders.

"Vá alí ao cofre!"

The manager started to move slowly, jerkily, towards the metal box embedded in the wall.

"Not that one," Pedro snapped. "Don't try to jerk me around. I am Big-Time P . . . Take me to the main safe before I blow your bloody head off!"

"It's in the b-back room," the man stuttered.

"Then let's go to it," Pedro said.

He turned to the stocky man holding a kitbag and rucksack. It was right that Harry Smell should have such a menial job. Harry wasn't anything like as important to this operation as he, Pedro, was.

"Siga-me," he said.

The stupid bastard just stood there, probably rigid with the fear that he had showed right from the start.

143

"*Siga-me,*" Pedro said again, and this time he followed.

The safe, a grey metal one, was embedded in both the floor and the back wall. It was taller than Pedro and must have weighed several tons. It would have taken a crane to lift it out, but Pedro did not need a crane. He had a shotgun, and that was the most powerful thing in the world.

He looked at his watch – 09:00:45.

"Open it!" he ordered.

The manager took the key, inserted it in the top lock and turned until it clicked, then extracted it and repeated the same process on the bottom one.

"I have to dial the combination now," he said nervously, pointing to the circular lock in the centre of the safe.

He had to kneel down to do it. Pedro put the shotgun to his head. He could feel the vibrations as the man shook.

"Do not be too long," he said, "or I just might pull the trigger."

Maybe once the manager had opened the safe, he would do it anyway, just to show him who was boss.

The manager's shaking hand turned the dial first to the left, then to the right, then back to the left again. Finally he sighed and stood up. He grasped the handle of the door, pulled down and then outwards. Nothing happened.

09:01:50

"What's the matter?" Pedro demanded.

"I must have dialled incorrectly."

"Do it again, and don't make a bloody mistake this time."

The manager knelt down again.

"Please," he said, "I can't concentrate with that gun against my head. Couldn't you take it away?"

Who did this bastard think he was? Pedro felt his finger

tighten on the trigger. And then Harry was standing by his side, a finger pointing down desperately at his watch to show the precious seconds ticking away.

"All right," Pedro said, and stepped backwards so that his gun was no longer in contact with the manager's skull.

The dial was turned again, the handle pulled, and this time the door swung open to reveal shelf upon shelf of lovely money.

09:03:10

Pedro pointed to the rucksack that Harry was holding open.

"Fill it," he said.

The manager, his years of training over-riding all else, picked up some bundles of notes and laid them neatly in the corner of the sack. Pedro stuck the shotgun in his face and pressed so that the man's nose tilted upwards.

"You think we mind if it gets creased?" he snarled. *"Mais rápido!"*

The terrorised manager began flinging money into the sack as fast as he could. When it was full to the top, Pedro pressed it down with his foot, and the manager added more.

09:04:17

"Now the other bag," Pedro said.

They should already be gone, but he could not bring himself to leave any of that beautisful money. Harry looked as if he was about to protest – but he couldn't, not without revealing that he was not Portuguese but English. Not without blowing the plan.

The bag was smaller, and took less time to fill. And still, there was money in the safe. While Harry put on the rucksack, Pedro took a few bundles and stuffed them down his trousers.

09:05:11

"Vamos," Pedro said.

The scene in the main office was exactly as he had left it, Frankie and Tony-Boy with their shooters, the clerks with their hands in the air. Pedro nodded to Frankie. Giving orders again!

The two made their way to the door, stood with their backs against the jambs, then burst out of the bank, twisting as they went, so that Pedro's gun covered the north end of the street and Frankie's the south.

Word had got round. A few people were watching, but they had been wise enough to keep a safe distance. The two gunmen swung in a half-arc, checking the centre of the road and the other side of the street. Nothing. Pedro whistled and Harry came running out of the bank, closely followed by Tony. As Tony started the car, Harry loaded the bags into the boot.

The policeman came out of a side street. He was fat, middle-aged, and was waddling rather than running, but the gun in his hand was real enough. He got within range and stopped, lifting his revolver to take aim. Pedro swung his shotgun in the direction of his middle, and let him have it with both barrels. Instantly, the man dropped to the ground.

"Got you, bastard-pig," Pedro said gleefully.

"Let's get out of here!" Frankie shouted.

The voice was high-pitched and tight. It didn't sound like him at all, and even in the heat of the moment, Pedro wondered what was wrong. And then he knew. Frankie Mason was scared – scared, while he, Pedro Gomes, was calm and in perfect control.

A scrap lorry trundled past, its driver, white faced, gazing down at the scene. Pedro wished he'd had time to re-load.

Frankie scrambled into the back of the car, Pedro into the front. Tony gunned the engine, and they shot off down the street. They were just about to overtake the lorry when the driver deliberately slued it across the street, blocking their path.

The wall of steel and rubber was only metres away from them. Pedro could see individual scratches on the paintwork, could almost read the manufacturer's name on the tyres. They were going to plough into it. They were all going to die. He closed his eyes.

He felt a great wrench as Tony pulled frantically on the wheel, he heard the screech of the tyres, he smelt burning rubber.

He opened his eyes again. The lorry was to one side of them, but ahead was the plate-glass window of a cafe. Tony had his foot down hard on the brake, but nothing could stop them now. They bounced up the curb, and crashed through the window.

The car stalled. Around it, showers of glass plummeted to earth. Behind it, the lorry's gears growled as the driver prepared for a fresh onslaught. Tony turned the key and the car coughed and missed. Frankie wound down his window and pointed the shotgun out. The engine refused to catch for a second time. Frankie fired at the back tyres of the lorry, shredding them. The car's engine ticked over and Tony backed, the tyres crunching broken glass, bit of masonry falling heavily on the roof.

There was no way past the lorry, Pedro thought. His opinion was obviously shared by the driver. As the car bumped off the pavement, Tony already had a tight lock on, so that they could go back the way they had come – down the one-way street.

Tony switched on the lights and pressed down on the horn. The battered Golf skidded and bumped its way into the oncoming traffic. One tyre was flat, Pedro realised – at least one.

An Opel mounted the curb to get out of their way; a Volkswagen Polo and a Mini Cooper, one only slightly behind the other, stopped dead on different sides of the road, and Tony drove a dog-legged path between them; a new BMW went into rapid reverse and almost made it into a side street before the Golf caught it a glancing blow.

And then, miraculously, they were clear, heading along the road that led to the Museum of Sacred Art. Pedro could see the third car Arnie had parked the day before, a Nissan Almera. It was standing in a quiet alcove. There was no one around. He still felt shaky, but he was getting better by the second.

The car stopped and the team got out. While Pedro slipped off his ski-mask, loose trousers and jumper, Frankie and Harry transferred the rucksack and kitbag to the Almera, and Tony started its engine. Pedro got behind the wheel. He smiled at the three masked faces.

"Good luck, fellers," he said, and then he was away, heading for the mountains.

The other men did not stop to watch his progress. They stripped off their clothes too, revealing the less conspicuous garments they were wearing underneath. Another car pulled up, and they quickly transferred to it the remaining contents of the boot. It drove away. They headed off in three different directions. Soon, each had joined the woman who had been waiting for him, and they were a gang no more, just three independent couples taking an early morning stroll.

Thirteen

C onstable Alberto Marques of the Policia Florestal arrived deliberately early that morning. He brushed aside Constable Barbieto's friendly greeting, and went straight to his post.

"You still have half an hour's duty to do," he reminded the other man, in icy tones, "but now I am here you may go."

It was his way of showing that he was not a minute-counting, petty-minded time-server – like some people he could mention.

The day before yesterday had been his birthday, and because everyone had insisted on buying him drinks – which it would have been rude to refuse – he had not got to bed until well after midnight. He had overslept the next morning, that was only natural, and had arrived at work a little late. Well, two and a half hours late. His head had been full of excuses and apologies for Barbieto; but they had not been necessary, because at nine o'clock, when his shift officially finished, the bastard had gone home, leaving the roadblock completely unmanned. If their superiors had found out, they could both have been in serious trouble. So Marques was not about to forgive his colleague – not quite yet.

He heard a car in the distance, coming up from Funchal.

There was no need to stop vehicles from that direction. He could have pulled up the pole then, but it was far better to wait until the vehicle appeared, so that the driver could see his Forest Police working for him.

The car hove into view, a Nissan Almera. Marques strode smartly towards the pole. What a difference there was, he thought, between the crisp, efficient way he raised the barrier and the slovenly way Barbieto did it. It was not being a slave to the clock that made you a real policeman.

It took him a second to realise that the Almera, far from slowing down, was actually accelerating. He waved his hands wildly, but the car continued to pick up speed. He jumped out of the way and watched, in amazement, as the car struck the barrier with a resounding crack. The pole groaned and then broke in two. The car skidded to the side, corrected itself, and then shot off into the distance.

The pole was Policia Florestal property, and had been ruined. Constable Marques ran to his Land-rover and set off in hot pursuit. It was only when he reached Poiso, where there was a crossroads and hence three possible routes the car could have taken, that it occurred to him that he should radio in the incident.

"A bank robbery!" Silva's voice sounded unusually high-pitched, almost hysterical. "A bank robbery here on Madeira. It's impossible!"

Gower looked down the street. The scrap lorry's back axle had been jacked up and a mechanic was taking off the shredded tyres. Outside the café, the waiters were sweeping up the shards of glass and pieces of rubble. And the area was swarming with policemen – questioning bank employees and the drivers of the cars which the Golf had met head-on; examining the Renault, still parked outside the bank; diverting traffic and shooing away sensation seekers.

It was nine thirty and no more than pleasantly warm, but beads of sweat were clearly visible on Silva's brow, and great damp patches were forming under his armpits.

"Impossible!" he said again.

"Of course it's not bloody impossible," Gower snapped. "It's bloody happened."

"What am I to do, Ron?" Silva asked desperately.

"What have you done already?"

"I have had the airport and harbour closed and I have men out looking for the getaway car."

And you haven't a clue what to do next, Gower thought. You pathetic little wanker!

A pick-up truck with the spare tyres for the crippled lorry edged its way around the police barrier. Someone was taking a hammer to the pieces of glass still embedded in the café's window frame.

"Ron," Silva said, "I have no experience of this kind of thing. Will you help me?"

He wanted to. Oh, he really wanted to, but he needed to settle the ground rules first.

"I'm on holiday, José," he said. "Besides, I've got out of the habit of taking orders from other people."

"It would not be like that, Ron. We would be partners."

Gower scratched his head. "No," he said reflectively, almost lazily, "it wouldn't work. The only possibility would be if you let me take complete charge, unofficially like. You'd have to gave me your assurance, before we even started, that whatever I needed to do you'd back me all the way."

Silva looked defeated. "All right," he said miserably.

Gower was suddenly all business. "What can you tell me about the robbery?"

"Four men, all masked. Only one of them spoke."

"Portuguese?"

"Yes, but not from Madeira. The manager said he did not have a Lisbon accent, he sounded more like a country boy. They used two cars. Three of them came in the Golf, the other," he pointed across the road, "in that Renault Megane."

When he had first heard about the robbery, Gower had prayed it was Mason. Sawn-off shotguns, ski-masks – it sounded just like the kind of job Frank would be involved in. But it was simply not Frank's MO. He hit the bank with three men and left the driver – Tony Horton – in the getaway vehicle. He had never been known to use two cars. Why the bloody hell would *anybody* use two cars?

"Get on to Lisbon," he said to Silva, "and have them fax out photographs of all bank robbers known to be operating on the mainland. Issue your men with the pictures, and then get 'em on the street. I want all hotels, holiday apartments, time-shares – everything – fully checked out. And while you're at it, do a cross-reference on the names to see if any of the mainland villains have got relatives living in Madeira. If they have, pull 'em in for questioning."

If only it could have been Mason! He'd really have had the bastard this time.

"Bloodys bastards luck, bloodys bastards luck," Pedro muttered to himself over and over again as he drove along the road to the Pico de Arieiro at a speed far in excess of the one Mason had instructed him to keep to.

Why had there been a roads block today? There had been

152

no roads block yesterday, when he was 'simulating actual conditions'. Bloodys bastards luck.

He screeched to a halt in the cafeteria car park, opened the boot and shouldered the rucksack. The timing had all gone wrong. He should have had half an hour to get round the curve of the mountain before the cafeteria opened and there was any chance of him being seen. But the police would already be looking for him. And it was vital he hid the money before he was spotted.

'*They can't prove a thing if they haven't got the money,*' Frankie had said.

He set off down the steps, trying to make better time than he had the day before, but the rucksack and kitbag slowed him down. He reached the vale and began to ascend again, and that was even harder work. The sweat trickled down his back and his breath was coming in short, sharp gasps.

The day before, he'd thought it a great honour to carry the money, but now it just seemed like a grind. And, for the first time, he began to wonder why he had been chosen for this particular job. Tony was a better driver, Frank was stronger. Even Harry Smell could have made quicker time along the trail. So why him?

He was almost at the bend when he heard the sound of voices further up the trail. Police? Already? No, one of the voices was a woman's and they were speaking in English. Hikers – and they were getting closer. He looked frantically around for somewhere to hide the money, but there wasn't anywhere. In desperation, he slid the rucksack off his shoulders and sat on it.

The speakers appeared round the corner. There were two of them, young and fit, dressed in shorts, T-shirts and stout hiking boots. Their faces were open and friendly. The man smiled at Pedro.

"Just taking a rest?" he asked.

"Yes," Pedro mumbled, "very tired."

He silently cursed himself for being so stupid. Why hadn't he pretended he couldn't speak English?

The man looked with interest at Pedro's kitbag and rucksack. He himself had only a small knapsack, which nestled comfortably at the base of his spine.

"You seem to be carrying rather a lot of equipment," he said.

Mind you own bloodys business, Pedro thought.

He wished he still had his shotgun with him.

"Must be jolly heavy," the woman said.

"Y – yes, but is necessary," Pedro stammered. "Are hammers and ropes. For rocks. I am a rock studier."

"Ah . . . I see," the woman said, sounding unconvinced.

Pedro wondered if it would be possible to push them both off the edge, then dismissed the idea. The man was too strong for him, and even if he managed to take him by surprise he would still have the woman to deal with, and she looked like she could put up a good fight.

The man seemed uncomfortable – embarrassed. "Well, goodbye," he said as he edged round Pedro, "and the best of luck."

"Yes, goodbye," the woman said, not even looking at him.

They'd take twenty minutes to reach the cafeteria. It would be open by then, so they'd probably stop for breakfast. And they would be likely to mention that they had met a strange man on the trail.

"Bloodys bastards luck," Pedro moaned, picking up his rucksack.

*　　*　　*

154

Gower surveyed the scene. The car was dented, one of its tyres was flat, the paintwork badly scratched. A sticker in the back window announced that it belonged to Avis Rent-a-car. But it was the other evidence, some in the car, some scattered around, which was interesting. There were four shotguns, four ski-masks, four black sweaters and pairs of over-trousers, and three zipper bags. The bags and trousers were all from Millets, the sweaters from Marks and Sparks.

Gower clicked his fingers. "Pen, paper!"

Silva came running with them.

Gower rested the pad on the roof of the police car and wrote down three rapid, accurate descriptions. He tore them off and handed them to Silva.

"Get these translated and distributed to your men on the streets," he said. "One of 'em's Portuguese, the other two are British. They won't be registered under their real names, but they'll be here somewhere."

The MO was all wrong, but the equipment fitted the bill exactly.

"Oh, Frank," Gower said happily, "however could you have been so bloody stupid?"

Fourteen

The easy chairs were removed and a gunmetal desk for Gower's use brought in. Silva's office still looked too much like a maiden aunt's sewing room for the Chief Superintendent's taste, but at least it had two telephones, one of which he commandeered.

He knew that Mason had used Portuguese Pedro on this job, and he always worked with Tony Horton, so that left one name missing. Gower flicked through his mental record of Mason's known associates and any other shotgun specialists he might have recruited. Willy Baxter? – no, he was doing time on the Moor; same with Jock McGuire except he was in Durham; Sid Cranshaw? – maybe; Harry Snell? – he was out, but from what they said, his nerve was gone; Phil Bolton? – possibly.

He jotted the likely prospects on a pad in thick, heavy handwriting, his pencil almost cutting through the top sheet of paper. What he really needed was access to proper files. He put through a call to London and was told that Scott was out.

"Well tell the idle young sod he'd better ring me as soon as he gets in," he ordered the duty sergeant. "And you'd better make sure that he does!"

Intimidation as a management technique, he thought as

he hung up. It was the only way to get things done – at least, the only way that he knew.

The phone rang on the other desk, jolting Silva out of his terrified stupor. But as the call progressed, his voice became more animated and his eyes grew brighter.

"That was the Policia Florestal," he said. "A car, a Almera, containing only a driver, crashed their roadblock on the way to Santana about half an hour after the robbery. The two things have to be connected."

Despite himself, Gower was impressed. "You were bloody quick getting that set up," he said grudgingly.

Silva looked suddenly sheepish. "It was not there for bank robbers. It was to stop the Christmas-tree . . ." he groped around for the right word, " . . .rustlers."

"Christmas-tree rustlers?"

"Near Christmas, there are people who go up into the mountains, with lorries, and cut down the trees," Silva explained. "That is why the Policia Florestal . . ." he trailed off.

Christmas-tree rustlers! Forest Police! What a bleeding set-up!

Gower stood up and walked over to the map behind Silva's desk. "Where exactly was this roadblock?" he asked.

"There," Silva replied, pointing to a wavy line high in the serra.

"And what's to stop the rustlers from going the other way, to San Roque or Santo da Serra?"

"There are roadblocks there too."

"In other words," Gower said, "we've got the bastard bottled up. He's either still on the this stretch of road between the blocks," he traced it with his finger, "or he's turned off here to Pico do Arieiro, which is a dead end."

"I'll get some men up there now," Silva said, reaching for the phone.

Brilliant! Gower thought to himself. I wonder why I never come up with good ideas like that. "And while you're at it," he said, "see if any of the agencies have rented a Almera today. And if they have, who to."

Silva had no sooner put the phone down than it rang again. This was how Gower liked it – thick and fast.

"The two cars," Silva said, "the Renault and the Golf, they were both rented by an Englishman, the day before yesterday. His name was—"

"Arthur Blake," Gower supplied.

"How did you know that?"

Because it explained exactly what Arnie the Actor was doing in Madeira, and why he had been using an alias. "Where is he?" Gower asked. "Down in the cells?"

Silva shrugged uncomfortably. "I don't know."

"You don't know! I told you to pick him up last night."

"You said he would be here for a week, and we have only skeleton staff at night, so I thought . . . I will have him brought in now."

"You'll be too bloody late," Gower said. "He wasn't part of the actual robbery, that's not his style, so he'll be long gone by now. Don't worry. Arnie is a louse, and he'll crawl straight back into his own woodwork – which is London. My lads will pick him up."

So now he knew about four of them. The net was closing. "If you can get out of this one, Frank," he said to himself, "you'd better change your name to Harry-sodding-Houdini."

As a man of business, Francisco Reis, Chief Cashier at the Banco do Lisboa, deplored the fact that the bank was closed for the rest of the day because of the robbery. As a handsome bachelor, still under thirty, he saw it as an unexpected bonus, an extra opportunity to try to inveigle one of the shapelier tourists into his bed. And there was one, just across the street, gazing into a shop window. Look at those legs! Look at that arse!

The woman turned and he realised that he knew her. Not only knew her – had slept with her. No wonder the legs looked familiar – they had spent enough time wrapped around his body.

He was just about to go over and grab her around the waist when he was hit by a thought that froze him in his tracks. What was she doing back so soon?

He remembered the comments in the bank, less than an hour earlier:

'They certainly struck lucky when they chose this bank.'

'Yes, they wouldn't have got half so much anywhere else. Think they were tipped off?'

'Of course not! We're all honest men here.'

And then he remembered further back, to last summer. Linda lying naked on the bed, and him leaning over her.

'Oh yes,' – as he kissed her glorious breasts – 'I'm only the Chief Cashier, but that's better than being the manager of most banks in Funchal. Most of them are small-time when compared to us. We handle most of the hotels. A lot of the businesses as well.'

She had seemed so impressed, he had told her everything. And now, today, the day the bank had been robbed, she was back again. It couldn't be chance.

Linda turned around and looked across the road. For a second, Reis was afraid that she had seen him, but when she crossed the street she went straight into the gift shop three doors up. She emerged again ten minutes later, a large parcel under her arm, and headed along the Avenida Arriaga. Reis followed her. He could not explain to himself exactly what he hoped to achieve from this, but his mind was in a panic and it seemed to help to be doing something.

At the end of the Avenida Arriaga, Linda took the Avenida do Infanta up to the Savoy Hotel. By the time Reis entered the hotel, she was already at the reception desk, with her back to him. He moved quickly across the lobby and hid behind the rotating newspaper rack, only a couple of metres away from her.

"Room Two-O-Seven," she said, and he could tell by the look of ecstatic confusion on the clerk's face that she had favoured him with one of her sexiest smiles.

She took the key and walked slinkily towards the lift. Most of the male eyes in the place followed her progress. And then she was gone.

Reis went straight to the bar and ordered himself a brandy. He now not only knew she was on the island, he had found out exactly where she was staying. The big question was – dare he tell the police?

The sun was getting hotter, the rucksack heavier. It seemed to Pedro as if some malevolent god had, overnight, moved the hiding place he'd selected another ten kilometres up the trail.

It was only fear that kept him going. The robbery had been easy, shooting the policeman just like aiming at a row of ducks in a fairground booth. But ever since then, ever since he had been alone, the fear had been growing until now it almost engulfed him. In his mind, his heavy footsteps beat out the rhythm of a solemn judge summing up.

'Ped-ro Gom-es you have been found guil-ty of murd-er and ro-bb-ery . . .'

"They can't prove a thing if they don't have the money," he chanted, obliterating the image of the courtroom from his imagination.

He reached the hiding place at last. The kitbag went in easily, but when he placed the rucksack in the fissure, and pushed, nothing happened.

"Bloodys bastard rucksack!" he shouted. "Bloodys arse-holes!"

He pressed down more heavily. If he couldn't get the rucksack in, then he would have to take the money out of it. Was the hole waterproof? He heaved, and it slid down, landing with a heavy plop at the bottom.

He reached into the fissure and found that he could not touch the rucksack. He looked down and saw only darkness. He collected up the small rocks he had gathered the day before and piled them into the hole. The money was perfectly, beautifully hidden. He felt safe at last.

The journey back was easier now that he was free of his burdens. Within minutes he had reached the corner of the mountain, and as he rounded the bend he could see the tour buses and a cluster of tiny figures standing at the viewpoint. He couldn't take the Almera back to Funchal, they would be looking for it, but it should be easy to make up a story about his car breaking down, and hitch a ride with another motorist. In an hour or so, he would be lying in a hot bath, soaking his aches and pains away.

He thought it was the sun reflecting off the car roofs at first, but the sun did not flash blue. The police had found the Almera.

The fear returned, but was soon smothered by a familiar, soothing voice. 'Somebody in Funchal might see the car change-over,' Frankie had said, 'so it's always possible that the police will find the second car in the cafeteria park. Right? Don't worry. There's a reason I've chosen that particular place to hide the money.'

There was a back-up plan. With Frankie, there was always a back-up plan. Pedro turned and started to walk back up the trail.

The police constable, one leather-booted foot resting on a large rock, passed the binoculars to his sergeant.

"He's not dressed for hiking," he said, "and when he got close enough to see our cars, he turned around. It has to be the man."

Silva was jabbering away in Portuguese on the telephone. Gower could not understand the words, but he knew that the Inspector was being placatory – wet. It was frustrating not knowing exactly what was being said, and he wished somebody would force all the wogs to learn a decent, civilised language.

Silva placed the phone back on its cradle. "That was our Director of Tourism," he said. "He wants me to open the airport again."

"And you told him to piss off."

"I . . . I asked him to give me a little more time."

"A little more time?" Gower exploded. "Listen, I think I know who did this job, but I can't be sure. And even if it is them, what's to stop them putting on some sort of disguise, using fake passports, and slipping out on the first available flight?"

"I could have men at the airport, looking out for them."

"Ah yes," Gower said. "The crack Portuguese CID –

clowns, idiots and dickheads. They couldn't catch a bleeding cold. The only chance you've got of nabbing these bastards is to keep them bottled up. You can't open the airport again."

Silva shrugged helplessly. "I may have to," he said. "Look, Ron, we are expecting ten planes today, ten planes full of passengers. They will demand the rooms they have booked, and they will get them. But what will happen to the people who are vacating their rooms today? Where will they sleep?"

"But a serious crime has been committed!"

"This I know, but tourism is very important to the economy of this island. If we get a bad name, we are in big trouble. I could hold off the Director for a while, but eventually he will complain to the authorities in Lisbon. They will instruct my superiors to unlock the airport, and there will be nothing I can do." He put his hands together almost in prayer. "Our only hope is to catch the robbers soon."

As if by divine intervention, the phone rang again. Silva's jabbering was very different this time – excited and hopeful.

"We've got them," he said, "or one of them anyway. The man in the Almera has been seen on the mountain track leading from the Pico do Arieiro."

Gower examined the map. The trail went on for miles without any side tracks, any way of escape. Silva was right for once. They did have the bastard. "Call out the helicopters," he said.

They could be there in ten minutes, the Almera driver could be back in the police station, having his knackers crushed, in less than half an hour.

"We . . . er . . . don't have any helicopters," Silva replied.

No bloody helicopters!

"There's an army base here, isn't there?"

"Yes."

"Well, use theirs."

"I don't think they have any either," Silva said apologetically. "The base here is mainly for training local conscripts. What do farm boys need flying machines for?" He brightened. "There is a real army base on Porto Santo. They could probably come."

A real army base! Nothing was real in this bloody country.

"All right," Gower said, "but get the army out searching the mountains anyway. If they're all local boys, they should know how to bleeding well handle themselves up there."

Gower's own phone rang. It was Scott calling from London – at last. "Mason didn't hire a second car in Madrid, sir," the sergeant said. "He was much cleverer than that. He got one of the local lowlife, a Victor Vidabaja, to hire it instead. Then Victor drove Mason's car to Barcelona and he used Victor's to get to Portugal. They only found it an hour ago, and even then it wasn't the Portuguese police who discovered it."

Well it bloody wouldn't be, would it? "Who did find it?" Gower asked. "The car-hire firm?"

"Yes, sir. Avis. They noticed it because it had Spanish plates and it was parked—"

"Outside Lisbon Airport," Gower interrupted. "And then the police finally got off their arses and found out that Mason had taken a flight to Madeira. Correct?"

"Er . . . yes, sir," Scott said lamely.

"Sorry to spoil your surprise, but thank you anyway, sergeant. You've been a great help," Gower said sarcastically. The line crackled. "Have we been cut off?"

Anything was possible with bloody Portuguese telephones.

"No, sir. I can still hear you."

"I want photographs of Mason, Horton and Portuguese
Pedro faxed here immediately. There's another one, but I
don't know who yet. And don't do it yourself, I've got a
more important job for you. Pick up Arnie Hebden – Arnie
the Actor. He was here yesterday, hiring the cars for a job
Mason pulled this morning."

Scott whistled softly. "Can you prove that, sir?"

"No, of course I can't bloody prove it. That's your job.
Put him through his paces. Tell him we've got the rest of the
gang and his only chance of a light sentence is to come clean
now. Rough him up a bit. Only – get results. Quick!"

He slammed down the phone.

A secretary entered and handed a note to Silva. The Inspector scanned it, and then smiled broadly. "The Portuguese police
are not so bad after all," he said. "We have found out where
another one of your gang, the one you say drove the getaway
car, is staying. He is not there now, but he and his wife have
a room at the Sheraton."

The Portuguese police were not so bad after all! They
were a bleeding joke! Tony was not married, and even if
he had been, did Silva really think that he'd take his wife
along on a job, as if it was a works' outing? Silva's men had
obviously pounced on the first man they came across who
vaguely resembled the description he had given them.

"What makes you so sure you've got the right man?"
Gower asked.

"Because," Silva smirked, "he is registered under the
name of Antony Horton."

Fifteen

P rivate Henrique held the rifle by its barrel, making sure
that the stock was pressed firmly against the floorboards
of the truck. The gun was not loaded yet, but once they
reached the Pico de Arieiro they would be issued with live
ammunition. And not just to shoot at a stupid target on a
range – they would be hunting a man, a desperate criminal
who had used a shotgun earlier in the day, and might still
be armed.

The trucks stayed in convoy until they hit the main road,
then some went one way, some of them the other. The
conscripts had not been briefed on the overall plan – nobody
ever told conscripts anything – but Henrique, who knew the
mountains well, could work it out for himself. The trail from
the Pico de Arieiro ran straight to the Pico Ruivo, so if they
could get men to both ends in time, all they had to do was
close in on the robber, like the two arms of a nut-cracker.
Ah, but what if he got to the Pico Ruivo before they did?
Then he had the choice of several trails.

So the Major, in his wisdom, had decided to cover all
contingencies. Squads would be sent to Santana, San Roque
and Curral das Freiras. Henrique was delighted that his truck
was going to the Pico de Arieiro. The conscripts heading for the
north of the island had a three-hour journey in front of them, up

narrow, twisting roads cut out of the mountainside. He would be in action in only half an hour. It was like being a real soldier.

Pedro knew that speed was the only thing he had on his side. "Push harder, push harder," he told himself, as the trail climbed first sharply up then slanted giddily down.

But he was out of condition, and his stops to catch his breath became more and more frequent. Nor was he properly shod. He could feel the sharp stones poking through the thin soles of his shoes and he knew that he was getting blisters. When he reached the first tunnel, crudely hacked through the living rock, he realised that he should have brought a torch. He had a box of matches in his pocket, but the wind blew out the first two or three, and he had no choice but to grope his way, agonisingly slowly, through the total blackness.

At Pico Ruivo, he turned north. He had gone less than a kilometre when he met a group of German hikers, dressed in lederhosen and carrying stout walking sticks. They nodded to him amiably enough, but looked questioningly at his clothing, which was more appropriate to a stroll in Funchal than a hard trek in the mountains.

"Frankie didn't think of that," Pedro thought angrily. "Bloodys bastard!"

The Germans would be bound to tell the police in which direction he was going, so he was forced to give them time to get clear and then turn round and head for Curral. It was the only intelligent thing to do, but he still fretted over the fact that it had cost him half an hour. It was past one o'clock, and he was still a long way from safety.

The harbour was full of angry fisherman who had planned to go in search of sharks, and furious sailors who were missing a favourable wind. Passengers had disembarked from a cruise liner early in the morning, and were now being told that though they could return to the ship, they must first be searched, and the ship itself could not move until further notice.

Things were even worse at the airport. There were over eight hundred people waiting to leave, and some of them had been there since seven thirty in the morning. They felt crowded in, tired and angry. There was no longer a queue which stretched right out of the airport cafeteria because the place had run out of both food and drink, and fresh supplies had not arrived. There was no longer a queue outside the toilets – they had become so foul that only the most desperate were using them.

And to make matters worse, all these frustrated people could see planes – the ones that were to take them back home – leaving empty.

Anyone in any kind of uniform was accosted by complaining passengers. A postman, who had come only to empty the airport mailbox, found his way blocked by a man who opened his suitcase and flung the contents into the air.

"See, I'm not a bank robber," the demented would-be traveller shouted, as his shirts and trousers swirled round him. "No money at all. I spent it all on your lovely bloody island. Can I go home now, please?"

Two or three fights started for no other reason than that tempers were frayed and people wanted to lash out at something – anything.

And the airport officials, surveying the scene but helpless to do anything about it, knew that things could only deteriorate.

Gower had all the registration slips from all the hotels spread out on the desk in front of him. Tony Horton had used his real name. Christ alone knew why – if they could furnish Arnie with a fake passport, surely they could have done the same for Mason's lieutenant? But given that Tony hadn't employed an alias, it was possible that some of the others hadn't either. And the only way to find out was to work laboriously through the cards.

It had been a long time since Gower had done such menial work himself, but there was no one else he could delegate the task to. He alone on the island would recognise the name of an English criminal when he saw it.

The phone rang, and Silva jumped nervously. He picked it up, and listened intently. "My men at the Pico have talked to two English hikers," he said, holding the phone away from his mouth. "They passed the man we are looking for on the trail. He had a large rucksack and a big bag."

"The money," Gower said excitedly. "How heavy did the bags look?"

Silva spoke into the mouthpiece again. "Very heavy," he said. "The hikers commented on it. He told them he was a geologist."

Gower studied the map. "We know when he crashed through the roadblock," he said, "and we know when your men spotted him returning to the cafeteria. He can't have got that far in the time in between. Put some of the army on the job of searching the first couple of miles of the trail, every bloody inch of it. The money's got to be there. Tell them you'll have their balls if they don't find it."

Things were happening very fast indeed. Gower returned to his registration cards, and the next name on the list was Harry Snell's.

Since he followed Linda into the Savoy, Francisco Reis

had spent his time drinking and trying to come up with a solution to his problem.

At eleven o'clock, he said to himself, "I will accuse her face to face and see how she reacts. If she says she is innocent, and I believe her, then there is no difficulty. If she says she is guilty, or she says she is innocent and I think she is lying, then that is the time to think about what to do next."

But bank robbers were dangerous people. Maybe she would tell her friends what he had said, and he would end up at the bottom of the harbour.

At a quarter to one, he said, "I will do nothing. I will pretend that the nights we spent together never happened – and no one will ever know."

Yet the robbers were bound to be caught – there was no escape from the island. Then they would be questioned.

'How did you know there was so much money in the bank?'

'The Chief Cashier is very indiscreet in bed.'

And surely it would go worse for him if he had not already admitted it.

By ten to three, after a great deal of soul-searching and many glasses of brandy, he decided to throw himself on the mercy (and discretion) of the Policia Judicial.

It was half-past three when Pedro reached Curral das Freiras. His body was aching, his head throbbing. He wanted to lie down where he was and sleep for a long, long time. Yet he dared not stop, because the army was out looking for him. On the trail down from the Pico he had heard them coming, just in time to slip behind a rock.

There were buses in Curral. Taxis, too. He was tempted to take one. But the army would be on the roads as well.

They would stop every bus and taxi and ask the inevitable questions: Where have you been? How long were you there? How did you get there in the first place? And he looked suspicious. He was dirty, his clothes were ripped, he had grazed his hand and his cheek.

There was no alternative to the levada that ran from Curral to Funchal. It would take him several hours, part of it would be in the dark and he might run into soldiers, but it was the best chance he had.

"Bloodys bastard luck," he said, limping painfully on.

Arnie the Actor sat across the table from Sergeant Scott. He was wearing a jacket that was square-cut with wide lapels and padded shoulders and wide trousers with turn-ups. His broad-brimmed hat was hanging behind the door. When Scott had found him sitting – bold as brass – in the Orinoco Club, he been drinking straight bourbon.

"So what d'ja want, copper?" he asked from the corner of his mouth.

"We've got Mason," Scott said, slowly and deliberately, "so we've got you."

"Never hoiyd of this Mason guy."

Scott rose from his chair and hit Arnie a backhanded blow that knocked him out of his seat. Arnie sprawled on the floor, blood trickling from his lip.

"You dirty rat," he said.

"Now don't you get abusive," Scott threatened, "And don't bugger about with me either, Arnie. You've been working with Frank Mason on a bank job. Until last night, you were in Madeira, setting it up."

Arnie picked himself up and wiped the blood from the corner of his mouth with the back of his hand.

"You can't pin nothin' on me, copper," he snarled. "I got an alibi."

"What!" Scott scoffed. "Twenty-four hours a day for the last three or four days?"

"Doesn't have to be twenty-four hours a day, wise-guy," Arnie said. "Only has to be one hour," he held up a single finger, "during the time you say I was out of town. Night before last I was playin' poker with Fat Sid the Bookie and Roadie O'Brien. You want alibis, copper," he leaned across the table and lowered his voice, "I got 'em – the best that money can buy. And now I wanna see my attorney."

Scott bounced Arnie off the wall for half an hour or so, being careful to cause pain without any bruising, but he knew he was getting nowhere. He could crack Arnie's alibi only by pulling in the witnesses and giving them an intensive grilling. And Gower's assertion that he had seen Arnie in Madeira wasn't ground enough for that – however much the Chief Superintendent might lament that things should be different. So they would have to get to Arnie through Mason, rather than the other way round.

He gave Arnie one last painful dig in the ribs. "You can go," he said, "but don't leave town."

"Don't worry, copper," Arnie said, as he made his way stiffly to the door, "ain't nobody born who can chase me outta my own burg."

At four o'clock, just as an empty British Airtours 707 had received clearance to take off, a crowd of about a hundred and fifty men, women and children, invaded the runway. Some stood around the wheels of the aircraft, shouting and shaking their fists, others lay down on the runway, directly in its path. There were many more police than was normal on duty at the airport, but they still needed to call in reinforcements from Funchal.

Some of the demonstrators allowed themselves to be herded away, others had to be physically carried. There were a number of scuffles and six people were arrested.

"Who cares?" one of those taken into custody called out. "Jail'll be an improvement on this."

By the time the Airtours plane took off, there were already two others circling the airport waiting to land – one of them running dangerously short of fuel.

"We have sent up army blankets and bedding," Silva moaned, "the big hotels are providing free meals, but they are getting angrier and angrier out at the airport. The Director says that even if we let them go now, it will be forty-eight hours before things are back to normal. I am under very heavy pressure."

"Patience, José," Gower said, showing uncharacteristic amounts of that quality himself. "Give it another couple of hours and we'll have the whole thing sewn up."

It certainly looked that way. One of Silva's men reported that the *maitre d'* of Jardim's Restaurant remembered Mason well, and had provided a full description of his companions.

"Tony Horton and Harry Snell," Gower murmured as he read it. "All together the night before a job. Bloody idiots!"

Gower and Silva conducted an interview with a nervous and remorseful Reis, who admitted that, yes, he had probably shot his mouth off too much about the bank's business to the girl; yes, she was back, and yes, she was in Room 207 at the Savoy, a room registered in the name of Mason.

By six o'clock in the evening, there was still no sign of

Pedro, and though they knew roughly where it was, the team of soldiers searching for the money had not yet uncovered it. But on the brighter side, plain-clothes men on duty reported that Mason, Horton and his woman, and the Snells, had arrived back at their hotels almost simultaneously.

"Why don't you go and pick 'em up?" Gower said.

Silva, warrant in pocket, was already moving towards the door.

Sixteen

"Mr Gower!" Mason said. "They got you across here quickly enough."

Gower indicated the chair facing him. "Sit down, Frank."

Mason ambled over and did as he had been told. He looked around at the dull green walls and high slit windows of the interview room.

"They're the same the whole world over, aren't they?" he asked. "My, what happy hours you and me have spent together in places like this."

You can be cocky, Frank, Gower thought. I don't mind. Because it's your bloody swan-song. You don't know just how much I've got on you.

He could have questioned one of the others instead. It would have been easier. But he didn't want things easy – he wanted to make Frank Mason crawl.

"It's more serious than usual," he said. "The policeman Pedro shot – he's dead."

Mason's mouth dropped open, and for the first time there was a trace of fear in his eyes. "He can't . . . it's not . . . Pedro's sho . . ."

That was it, Gower thought, the first breach in the dam. From now on the water would trickle through faster and faster until it became a flood, until the whole of Mason's self-esteem had been washed away – until he had been destroyed.

"What were you going to say, Frank?"

"Pedro shot a policeman? Pedro who?"

Good recovery, Frank, but not good enough.

"That's not what you were going to say, Frank. You were going to say that Pedro's such a wally that you'd never trust him with live cartridges, so you gave him blanks. Not like the ones you shot into the tyres of the lorry, eh?"

"Don't know what you're talking about, Mr Gower."

"And you're right, of course. The policeman isn't dead. He's like all the local cops – a gutless wonder. When he heard the explosion he dropped, and he stayed down until you were well away. But I'm not a greedy man, Frank. I don't have to get you for murder, I'll be happy with armed robbery."

He walked around the edge of the room, ending up behind the seated man. Four suspects out of five would have turned their heads so they could keep him in their vision, the fifth would have been so rigid with terror that he couldn't move. Mason didn't move, but there was no evidence of paralysed knotted tension in his shoulder muscles. Well, that would come. And in a way, the longer it took, the sweeter it would be when it finally arrived.

"You see, Frank," Gower continued, moving again to disorientate him, "the best kind of collar is when you catch the villains at the scene of the crime, shotguns still smoking in their hands. But second best is what I've got on you, when there's so much circumstantial evidence that we can build up a clear picture in the eyes of the jury even without a confession. And we will get a confession, make no mistake about that. Harry Snell or

Pedro will be only too glad to shop you to save their own necks."

He walked around in front of Mason again, so that he could see his face. There had been panic there earlier, but now his expression showed nothing.

"Let's start at the beginning, Frank," he said, "with the bunk you did from Spain. Not only was it illegal, driving a car you hadn't rented, but it'll look very suspicious in court."

"Oh, come on, Mr Gower," Mason said. "You're not even trying. So it was illegal. What'll I get? A fine? Three months max., if I'm prepared to go back to Spain – which I'm not. And as for how it'll look in court, my brief'll tear it to shreds." He grasped the front of his sports shirt between thumbs and forefingers and adopted a rich, plummy voice: "My client committed a youthful transgression over twenty years ago, a transgression brought on him by poverty and desperation. Since then, despite the fact that he has led an honest life, and never received so much as a parking ticket, the police have continued to persecute him. They would not even leave him alone when he went to Madrid, to improve his mind by studying the art treasures of the Prado. Is it any wonder that this man, sick of harassment, chose to exercise a little subterfuge in order to gain some peace? It was wrong, yes, but it was understandable."

"Very good, Frank," Gower said. "But you're missing the point. It's not the individual details on their own which matter, it's the complete picture they build up. You have three known criminals on a small island, criminals who actually have a meal in a posh restaurant together, and the very next day a robbery is committed and the robbers' physical descriptions match those of the happy diners. Bit of a coincidence, wouldn't you say?"

"Nothing wrong with three old friends having a meal together," Mason replied. "And even if one of the robbers did look at bit like me, well, a lot of people are over six feet these days – it's the powdered milk we were fed as kids."

"Three British criminals on the island," Gower continued, "and all the equipment used in the raid was British as well."

"It's good to know that even criminals are learning that British is best."

"Your little tart Linda was screwing the Chief Cashier at the bank," Gower pressed on, hammering another nail in Mason's coffin, "and she asked him a lot of probing questions. How d'you think that will look in a conspiracy charge?"

"She's always had a healthy appetite – for both information and sex."

"And finally, Frank, there's Pedro and the money. We haven't got either of them yet. You see, I'm being straight with you. I can afford to be, can't I? But we will pick up Pedro sometime tonight, and it's only a matter of time before we find where the little tosser hid the rucksack."

There was a barely perceptible twitch in Mason's left eye, but to Gower it spoke volumes. Mason was worried but it wasn't Pedro that was causing him concern, it was the money. Was he really so bloody stupid as to think they couldn't get a conviction without the loot? Or was he prepared to go away for a long stretch as long as he knew the money would be waiting for him when he came out – a sort of retirement plan.

Gower placed both hands on the table, palms down, and

leaned forward. "I'm going to be nice to you, Frank," he said. "I could easily go to Harry Snell or that girl Tony brought with him," – Mason's eyelid flickered again – "or I could wait until they bring Pedro in. But I'm going to give you first shot at coming clean and lightening your sentence. And do you know why? Because I like you."

Nothing could be further from the truth, and they both knew it. It was because Gower hated Mason that he was giving him this chance. It wasn't enough that he could put him inside. He wanted to see him grovel, ask favours. He wanted to see him go to prison knowing that he had shattered his own precious code of honour. He wanted to make it hard for Mason ever to live with himself again.

"I refuse to answer any more questions without my lawyer being present," Mason said flatly.

Gower felt rage bubbling up inside him. Who did this prick think he was – a knight in shining armour? He was nothing but a bank robber, a common criminal.

"Screw you, Mason!" he said.

He realised that he was standing upright again and that his right arm was lifted back ready to swing. The tightness had returned to his chest, too.

"I wouldn't do that, Mr Gower," Mason said quietly.

The arm froze in mid-air. "Where do you think you are?" Gower demanded. "This is a police station. You touch one hair on my head, and I'll have four uniformed men in here beating the shit out of you."

"I still wouldn't do it if I was you," Mason advised.

Gower felt the arm fall limply to his side.

"You're a mug, Mason," he said angrily. "I always knew that, but I never knew how far it bloody went. You'll get twenty years, maybe more under the Portuguese criminal code. And I wouldn't ask for bail if I was you, because when Ted Sims finds out about you and Linda, your life won't be worth a tinker's cuss on the outside."

He stormed out of the room.

Mason may have told Gower very little, but in comparison to the others, he was like a supergrass.

"I want to see a lawyer," Mary Snell said, her expression as tight as her permed hennaed hair.

"I . . . um . . . want to see a lawyer," mumbled Harry Snell, his eyes gazing at the floor, his fingers clasped tightly together, his hands shaking.

"It's no good shouting at me like that," Susan sobbed, the tears running down her cheeks, "I'm not going to say anything until I've seen a lawyer."

"I want a lawyer," Linda said, crossing her legs, "a male lawyer."

"Come on, Mr Gower," Tony drawled easily, "I'm entitled to a lawyer if I want one, and you'll get nothing out of me till then."

If they'd tried to come up with an alibi, he would have had something to work with, a structure of lies and evasions which he could have slowly, methodically, demolished. But they wouldn't say anything except lawyer, lawyer, bleeding lawyer.

The Mason gang were playing the game according to rules they had just invented, and refused to see that these rules simply would not work. Until he caught Pedro! Then surely they would understand it was all over.

It was at the highest point of the levada – a thin ribbon of concrete clinging to the mountainside a hundred feet above the ground – that Pedro saw the soldiers. There was nowhere to hide, nowhere to run except back the way he had come.

They were fresh, and he was exhausted and weak with hunger. They would soon catch him, unless he missed his footing and plunged to his death. He could see the barrels of their rifles glinting in the pale afternoon sun. They might not bother to follow him, maybe they would just use him as target practice. Even if by some miracle he managed to escape them, his clothing was no protection against the cold night air, and he would probably die of exposure. And there would be soldiers at the other end, too.

"Bloodys shit luck," he moaned as he limped up to the search party.

The policeman was the most terrifying person Susan had ever met. He had looked like an evil toad, squatting on the chair opposite and spitting his vile questions at her.

"You're nothing but a tart, isn't that right? Anybody with a couple of bob in his pocket can have you."

He had no real human feelings, she was sure of that, not just for criminals – for anybody.

"You don't like the way I speak to you, eh? Not respectful enough? Well, you lost the right to any respect when you became Tony's whore."

She hadn't wanted to cry, but the tears had come anyway, and when she wouldn't stop – couldn't stop – he had almost been on the point of hitting her.

"Where were you between half-past eight and half-past nine? What time did Horton leave? Did you see the gun? The ski-mask? Answer me, you little slag!"

Every time she had seen the ugly mouth flap open and known that more poison was about to dribble out, she had wanted to scream out the answers he had asked for. Just to make him go away. But she wouldn't, she wouldn't let Frank down, she wouldn't! Yet at the same time, she wished that neither he nor she were involved in any of this.

As they had marched him along the levada, two in front, one behind holding a rifle to his back, Pedro had thought only of his aching feet. On the truck journey back to Funchal it had been his hunger pains that had been bothering him. Now, in Funchal Central Police Station, all thoughts of mere physical misery had been replaced by an all-consuming terror. Gower was here! Sitting opposite him!

"We've got the whole gang, you know," the Chief Superintendent said conversationally. "Frank, Tony, Harry."

So the first part of the fail-safe had collapsed – they had discovered the gang wasn't Portuguese and pulled them in. But there was still the second part. Pedro kept repeating Frank's words over and over in his mind – a silent prayer. *'They can't prove a thing if they haven't got the money. They can't prove a thing if they haven't got the money.'*

"What were you doing up there in the mountains, Pedro?" Gower demanded.

"I go for a walk."

"All day?"

"Yes. I start out before the bank robbery."

"What bank robbery?" Gower asked, pouncing like a cat on an unsuspecting sparrow. "How do you know anything about a bank robbery if you've been in the mountains all day?"

"I meet some other walkers," Pedro said, improvising. "They tell me about it."

"The policeman who was killed," Gower said. "A lot of witnesses think that you did it. On the other hand, Frank was standing next to you at the time. Perhaps we could produce

182

some people who saw him do it – and forget the others. If you're prepared to co-operate."

Pedro licked his lips nervously. It was tempting. He would get a lighter sentence for robbery than he would for murder. But maybe Gower couldn't put them away anyway.

They can't prove a thing if they haven't got the money.

"You're thinking about the money, aren't you?"

Pedro jumped, horrified at Gower's ability to see into his mind.

"Funny thing, you're friend Frank seems to be pre-occupied with the money too."

"What money, Mr Gower?"

The Chief Superintendent's fist was almost a blur as flew across the table and slammed into Pedro's stomach. The injured man slumped forward, his eyes watering, retching sounds coming from his throat. Through the wall of pain he heard Gower's voice as if it were coming from a very long way away.

"I'll tell you what money, Pedro. The money you carried along the mountain track – not far, because it was heavy – until you found a good place to hide it. But there aren't that many good places, Pedro, and we've got men out checking them all. We'll have it by morning at the latest."

If they found the money, Pedro thought as he clutched his stomach, it would be the end. If they found the money he would make a deal with Gower. But he would hold off until then – because there was just a chance they wouldn't find it.

There was still a light burning in Silva's office and the Inspector was at his desk, red-eyed, trembling, showing all the signs of imminent nervous collapse. When he heard the door open, he looked up hopefully.

"Nothing yet," Gower said. "But Snell will crack soon, even if Pedro doesn't."

"Have they asked for lawyers?"

"Yes," Gower growled. "They've done practically nothing else – but they're not bloody getting them."

"But they have a right to—"

"They asked, but nobody heard them. When they've told us something useful, then our deafness might go away."

Silva fumbled nervously with the paper clips on his desk. "Ron," he said, "I have had to lift the restrictions on the airport and the harbour."

"You've bloody what!"

"The order came directly from Lisbon. And does it matter? We have the men, and tomorrow we will have the money."

"No," Gower said tiredly. "I suppose it doesn't matter. All right, José. I'm going to get three or four hours sleep now, then I'll get back to it."

"What about the women? Can they leave?"

"Until I get the truth," Gower replied, "nobody leaves."

Seventeen

Mason was wearing chains, thick heavy chains that weighed him down as he climbed up the wooden steps to the gallows. His head was bowed and he was utterly defeated. By the gibbet, a black hood over his head, his eyes glinting evilly, stood the executioner. Although he seemed to be watching the scene from a distance, Gower knew that he himself was the executioner, that it was his eyes which peered out of the hood, his hands that would place the noose around Mason's neck.

The condemned man reached the top of the steps and then a strange, terrible thing happened. The executioner pulled off his hood and it was not Gower at all, but Tony Horton. He tugged at Mason's chains and they fell to the ground, and then the two men were running, escaping. Gower wanted to chase them but his legs would not move, however much he willed them to, however much . . .

Gower woke up in a sweat. He never slept well during serious investigations, but nightmares were new to him. He reached for the bottle of Teacher's on the bedside table and poured himself a generous shot.

Mason couldn't get away. He had him cold, even without a confession, even without the money. There was nothing Tony Horton or anyone else could do to save him this time.

He looked at his watch. It was time to go back to the police station and start putting the pressure on those bastards again. Maybe the money had turned up by now.

Private Henrique was pissed off. The previous afternoon it had all seemed like the start of a big adventure – and then what had happened? Other soldiers had caught the bank robber near Curral, and his squad, because they had been on the spot, had been lumbered with the job of looking for the robber's rucksack. A rucksack! How exciting could that be, even if it was full of money?

He stopped in front of a small niche in the cliff face. If he'd had his rifle, he would have pointed it in, but the sergeant had collected up the weapons as soon as the criminal had been apprehended, and he had to make do with his torch.

"All right, Rucksack," he called out, as the beam of light bounced off the rock, "I know you're in there. You haven't got a chance. Come out with your straps up."

He walked on until he reached the whitewash slash line that marked the end of his own territory. Beyond that he could see other conscripts, sluggishly shining their torches and peering into cracks.

"How many times have we been over the same ground?" asked his partner, Private Alves.

Henrique shrugged. "Five? Six?"

If they'd been their own masters, they'd have abandoned their search long ago. It was like when they'd been kids and had lost their ball in the long grass – after half an hour or so they'd give up and decide to buy a new one. But they were in the army now, and the sergeant had made it quite plain that until they found the rucksack, the search would continue, right through Christmas Eve and into Christmas Day.

Alves stopped at a fissure they had examined numerous times before, and peered in.

"Hey," he said, "I've found something!"

"What?"

Henrique's voice was suddenly full of anticipation. If it was the bloody rucksack, they could all go home.

Alves turned around, and there was a broad grin on his face. "Rocks," he replied. "Fancy finding rocks on a mountainside."

"Piss artist," Henrique said, and they moved on, leaving the rucksack and kitbag where Pedro had hidden them.

Special flights had been lifting the tourists off the island all night, and by mid-morning there was no more than a three-hour delay. The unmarried teacher who had been able to get away only because she had promised faithfully to have Christmas dinner with her mother, sighed with relief as she walked through passport control. The three women who had flown over to spend a few hours with their husbands after weeks of separation – and had ended up devoting more time to trying to sleep on the airport floor – followed her. At the back of the queue, the writer of pulp fiction glowered down at his desktop computer and thought of the weeks of work he had put into the idea of an unprecedented robbery on Madeira, wasted now that some selfish bastards had actually pulled one.

The authorities were still searching the passengers, just to be on the safe side, but not very thoroughly – a cursory glance through a suitcase was enough to tell whether or not it was crammed with thousand-escudo notes.

Things were returning to normal down by the sea, too.

Utilitarian fishing boats chugged out of the harbour with their cargoes of deep-sea sportsmen, each one quietly optimistic that today he would land a marlin so big that it would beat the island's record of 734 pounds. Sleeker, fancier craft were setting off for a day's sailing.

Jack Sodbury, sitting cross-legged on the fore deck of the *Seaspray*, watched it all with pleasure. There was a lot more to this sailing lark than met the eye. There was a lot more to the Skipper too, he thought, as he saw the striped-jerseyed figure emerge from the harbour master's office. He'd seemed like a chinless wonder at first, but the way he'd handled this boat was a pleasure to watch. They said Vancouvers were difficult boats to manage, that you needed an experienced crew. Well, none of the *Seaspray*'s crew was experienced, but under the Skipper's guidance they'd got here. And it hadn't all been plain sailing by any means.

He'd get a boat of his own when he got home, Jack decided. Not a big one like this, just something for pottering about in near the shore. Yes, there was certainly more to this lark than met the eye.

The Skipper was level with the boat now. "Good news, Jack," he shouted down. "I've talked to the harbour police and they say we can leave any time we're ready."

He descended the steps and placed his foot confidently on the deck.

"A very nice off-shore wind," he said. "Call Len and Phil on deck. I think we'll leave under sail. No real point in starting the engine, is there?"

Sodbury smiled to himself again. It would have been easier to leave under engine-power, but not half as much fun.

188

The wind was ahead of the beam. They raised the mainsail and released the shorelines. The boat drifted gently clear of the quay.

"Trim the mainsail," the Skipper ordered.

A month ago, none of the crew would have known what he was talking about. Now, they executed his command with practised efficiency.

"Hoist the headsail."

Another smooth operation.

"Trim the headsail."

The boat sailed out with stately grace. Sodbury looked back, watching the harbour get smaller, the Casino Park Hotel shrink until it was a tiny white box. What a lovely way to spend your time.

"It's a pleasure sailing with you, Skipper," he said.

"Thank you," Nigel Monk replied.

"We've found the money, Pedro," Gower said. "It's all over."

Pedro's eyes, wide with fear, darted from one end of the interrogation room to the other. "What money, Mr Gower?" he asked, when he made sure that there was no telltale rucksack lurking in the corner.

He's right, Gower thought to himself. If I had the money, it'd be on the table, right in front of him, where I could rub his bloody nose in it.

"Don't give me that shit!" he said aloud. "You know what sodding money. And you'd better tell me about it while you've got the chance."

"I want to see a lawyer," Pedro said.

"Take him back to his cell," Gower instructed the police-man escort.

Gower was tired, his back ached, and the tight band around

his chest refused to let up. It was two thirty in the afternoon, he had been interrogating non-stop since eight o'clock that morning. And getting bloody nowhere!

'I want to see a lawyer. I want to see a lawyer. I want to see a lawyer.' It was all the bastards ever said.

And not only them. Silva was bleating the same thing with ever-increasing urgency and panic. So far, Gower had been able to hold him off by sheer force of personality, but they were rapidly reaching the point at which Silva would become more frightened of the consequences than he was of his British colleague.

"Charge them," Gower said. "You've got enough evidence."

If he'd been in control, if this had been his patch, they would have been booked long ago.

Silva flapped his arms like a broken windmill. "We don't . . . I . . . if you could get one of them to confess . . ."

Bloody wimp!

Pedro was frightened of them finding the money, so was Mason. If only that would turn up, one of them would crack – Gower was sure of it. He wanted to be out there himself, tearing the mountainside apart with his bare hands.

"Isn't there a metal detector in the jeep?" Alves asked, scuffing with his boot the whitewashed line that marked the end of their territory.

"Yes," Henrique replied. "So what?"

"Why don't we use it?"

Henrique took a last drag on his cigarette and threw it over the railing. He watched it arc and then plunge downward in the direction of the valley. It was not even half way to the ground before he lost sight of it. He turned his mind to his friend's suggestion.

"Because, pea-brain," he said, "we're looking for paper money, not coins."

"I know," Alves replied, "but the money was in a rucksack. True?"

"True."

"And rucksacks have buckles and fastenings – which are made out of metal."

Henrique looked at his friend with new respect. "You're right," he said.

They went over the trail again, running the metal detector along the cliff face. By the time they reached Pedro's fissure, they had found a hundred escudos, a penknife and a lighter.

The reading in the gap was not very high. Henrique reached down and was just able to touch the top rocks with his fingertips. To remove them, he would have to bend over almost double and, working in that cramped space, his knuckles would soon be grazed and bloody.

"It's probably just a beer can," he said, listening again to the faint click of the detector. "Not worth the trouble."

They moved on again, the detector occasionally coming to life and leading them to minor, easily accessible treasures. They stopped at the white line and Alves added a second, more pensive scuff mark to his first. "Why would anybody pile a lot of rocks on top of a beer can?" he asked.

The two young men sprinted back to the fissure, Henrique beating his partner by a short head. He crammed his body into the confined space and, ignoring the damage to his hands, scrabbled for a grip on the rocks, twisting his body to pass them, one at a time, to Alves. He had removed six or seven when his fingers came into contact with cloth.

Gower looked at the dirty, scuffed bags resting on Silva's

desk. They had been discovered at half-past five, just as Silva, finally pushed beyond the point of endurance, was about to call a lawyer. And even their recovery seemed to have done little to stiffen the Inspector's spine. As he gazed at them now, his fingers played nervously with his droopy moustache.

"We ring the manager immediately," he said, "and he puts the money back in the bank."

"So somebody else, armed with a tin opener, can walk in and take it out again?" Gower asked. "No, of course we don't put it back in the bank. It's bloody evidence, isn't it?"

Christ, this bloke was a plonker.

He walked over to Silva's desk and began to unfasten the buckles on the rucksack. They were tightly secured; whoever had fastened them in the first place had made a good job of it, especially considering he'd done it in the heat of the bank raid. Still, that was sensible – you didn't want money blowing all over the mountainside.

"You get four men in here," he said, "four men you can trust – or at least four who are less light-fingered than the rest – and you get them to count the money and make a note of serial numbers at the beginning and end of each package."

"That will take all night," Silva said.

"Yes, it will probably take all bloody night."

Jesus, Silva wanted it easy. The little tosser had got somebody else to catch his criminals for him, and he was even complaining about doing the routine paperwork himself.

The buckles were all unfastened. Gower peeled back the flap of the rucksack – and froze. Oh, this would get Pedro talking all right! He would spill his guts when he saw this.

"You really are a bastard, Frank Mason, aren't you," Gower said to the empty air.

Eighteen

T he first things that Pedro saw, staring accusingly at him
from the centre of the interrogation-room table, were the
kitbag and rucksack.

They couldn't be the ones! It was some trick of Gower's!
But it was no trick, they were the very same bags he had
sweated and strained with along the mountain track.

'They can't prove anything without the money.'

Well, they had the money now, and he knew it was all
over. He knew, too, that despite the last two days, he was
not a tough gangster – that he was nothing more than a
village boy playing at being big.

"I make a deal, Mr Gower," he shrieked. "I tell you
everything. I don' want to go to prison for a long time."

He told of his recruitment by Arnie the Actor and the
meetings in the bed-sit. He described the robbery: how he
had held the shotgun at the manager's head, how Harry Smell
had filled the rucksack, how Frankie had shot out the tyres of
the lorry, how Tony-Boy had driven the wrong way down a
one-way street.

"Who loaded the money into the boot of the getaway car?"
Gower asked.

"Harry Smell. Frankie and me, we do the important work,
covering the street," Pedro answered, with just a trace of his

old arrogance.

"And who took the money out again, and put it in the boot of the Almera?"

"Frankie and Harry Smell. Tony-Boy is starting the Almera, I am getting out of my bank-robbings clothes."

Gower nodded as if satisfied. "And you've told me everything, Pedro?"

"Everything, Mr Gower. I swear on my grandmother's grave."

Gower brought his fist down heavily on the table. The rucksack wobbled. "Your grandmother's grave! They don't bury whores like your grandmother, they just chuck 'em out with the rest of the rubbish. Tell me about Mrs Snell and that tart Susan, you little shit!"

"Who? I don' understand."

"So you don't know about them. Of course, you weren't at the party."

"Party?"

"In Jardim's Restaurant, the night before the robbery. They were all there."

"Frankie never told me about no party. Frankie say we don' meet. Frankie say if we bumps into each other, we looks the other way."

Gower scowled. "There seem to be a lot of bloody things 'Frankie' never told you, don't there?" He stood up and walked to the corner of the room. "Well, you done it Pedro, you sold 'em all down the river, 'Frankie', 'Tony-Boy', the whole bleeding bunch of 'em."

"I don' care," Pedro moaned, "I don' care."

"You bloody well shouldn't," Gower said, "because they double-crossed you as well."

The Portuguese was not interested. What Mason had done,

or had been going to do wasn't important now. It mattered only that he had been caught and, even with the confession in his favour, would be spending the next few years in prison.

"Before you go back to your cell," Gower continued, relentlessly, "wouldn't you like to look at the money one last time?"

Pedro face was a blank, all emotion washed away.

"Go on, take a look," Gower urged him. "After all, it's the reason you got caught. And it must have been hard work carrying it along that mountain trail."

Pedro shook his head.

"Go to the rucksack, you lump of dog shit," Gower ordered, "and touch the money. Bring me some to have a look at, too."

Pedro was feeling too weak to fight. He walked to the table, as if in a daze, and lifted the flap, just as Gower had done earlier. His collapsed facial muscles suddenly sprang to life, and the expression they formed was one of anger and amazement. He dug his hands deep into the rucksack, tunnelling, throwing its contents all over the floor. He up-ended it, shaking all the bundles out, then kicked them, as if they were a pile of dead autumn leaves. Finally, when he was convinced that there was nothing else hidden in the bags, he picked up one of the bundles and waved it at Gower. "What the bloodys hell is this?" he demanded.

Gower took his impertinence with equanimity. "Inspector Silva tells me it's the Jornal da Madeira," he said, "neatly cut up to the size of Portuguese bank notes. All that struggling, all that effort, was for bits of old newspaper. Nice sodding friends you've got, haven't you?"

Gower stood on silently while Silva charged Mason, Horton and Snell with bank robbery; Mrs Snell, Susan and

Linda with complicity. They all repeated their requests to see a lawyer.

"Not until they tell us where the money is," Gower said to Silva, when they were alone.

"I have charged them, they must have an advocate," Silva replied, picking up the phone. "I will call Senhor de Sousa. His English is excellent."

"But is he a good lawyer?" Gower asked.

"He has high standing on the island."

"Then get somebody else," Gower suggested. "A beginner or a dead-beat shyster. Preferably somebody whose English will make even Pedro wince."

"Senhor de Sousa," Silva said – firmly for him – and dialled the number.

Senhor de Sousa was a tiny middle-aged man who was perpetually brushing imaginary specks off his immaculate jacket. He looked at the two policemen with sharp, suspicious eyes.

"A liberal," was Gower's instant classification, and the lawyer was slotted neatly into the Chief Superintendent's hierarchy of shit-bags, somewhere between pimps and drug pushers.

De Sousa went to see Susan first, but was gone less than two minutes. "Before she talks to me herself, my client wishes me to see Mrs Monk," he said.

"She's done nothing but whine about a lawyer for the last twenty-f . . . twenty minutes," Gower said, hastily amending his statement midway, "and now she's got one, she wants him to see Linda instead. What the bloody hell for?"

"It is not for you or I to question my client's instructions," de Sousa said coldly. "Will you please have me escorted to where you are holding Mrs Monk."

He spent twenty minutes with Linda, and then requested a meeting with Silva and Gower. "My client—" he began.

"Which client?" Gower demanded.

"My client, Mrs Monk, is prepared to make a statement," he said, "but only under certain conditions. She has been incarcerated in this police station for over a day and has not been permitted to consult a lawyer—"

"She never bleeding asked."

De Sousa shot Gower a look of contempt and disbelief. " . . .not permitted to consult a lawyer," he continued. "Before she makes a statement, she feels the need for a little fresh air. She would like to walk around the town for an hour or so. She is quite willing to be accompanied by a policeman."

"No!" Gower said. "I've never heard anything so bloody ridiculous in my life."

De Sousa ignored him and addressed his next remark exclusively to Silva. "I have certain information you do not," he said in measured tones. "In your own interest, Inspector, I would strongly advise you to agree to her request. Before this regrettable matter goes any further."

"Yes, yes," Silva said, scared shitless by de Sousa's attitude. "Yes, she can go for a walk. As long as she promises to talk after it."

Gower snorted with disgust. You just didn't treat criminals like that. When you had them down, you put the boot in.

And then it occurred to him that there might be another reason behind Linda's request. "All right," he said, "it's a good idea."

De Sousa looked at him with suspicion.

"A walk might clear her head, make it easier for her to give her statement," Gower explained.

When de Sousa left to tell his client that her request had

been granted, Gower grabbed Silva by the arm. "I want two policemen with her," he said, "the sharpest, most alert bastards you've got. And I want them to watch her every action. What she does, where she looks."

"But why?"

"For Christ's sake, man," Gower exploded. "It's bloody obvious. There can only be one reason for her wanting to go out now. She wants to make sure the money is still where they put it!"

Linda walked along the Avenida do Infante and through the park. She seemed quite relaxed, her guards reported later. She was just taking the air; not looking at anything in particular, not peering into any nooks or crannies or glancing behind any bushes, not feeling loose bricks in the wall or anxiously examining the flower beds for signs of fresh digging. When she had exhausted the possibilities of the park, she strolled along the sea front. She stopped at a bar and ordered drinks for herself and the two policemen. She drank her coffee and then informed her guards that she was ready to go back and make a statement.

Gower spent the time Linda was out racking his brains to discover a loophole that Mason and his gang could slip through, and could find none. In the jargon that had been current when he joined the Force, he had the robbers 'bang to rights'.

And yet Linda seemed perfectly calm when she returned. She sat on a straight-backed chair in Silva's office, her beautiful slim legs crossed, her skirt riding high. Gower noticed the police stenographer's eyes were almost popping out of his head, and was sure that Linda was putting on the show deliberately.

"Right, Linda," he said. "Do you want to tell us all about it?"

She smiled, a sexy, promising, open-lipped smile that had no effect on him. "What do you want to know?"

"We can start with what you were doing at the time of the robbery."

"When exactly was that?"

"You know when it bleeding well was!"

"Really," de Sousa said. "I must protest at the lang—"

"It's all right, Mr de Sousa," Linda said, her smile far from wasted this time, "I know Mr Gower's not a gentleman."

"It was at nine o'clock," Gower said through clenched teeth. He would get his revenge later.

Linda pretended to think, pursing her brow prettily. "Nine o'clock, nine o'clock . . . Let me see. I had a headache yesterday morning, but I went down for breakfast anyway. I was alone. Yes, that's where I was at nine o'clock. Because I didn't have my watch on and I asked one of the waiters the time. He said it was exactly nine and pointed to the clock on the wall. Silly of me not to have noticed it. I think he'll remember."

"I bet he bloody well will," Gower thought. Most men would remember Linda.

He saw her game now. What Mason had been expecting her to do was stay in the room, so that he could claim later that they'd been together. Instead, she'd gone downstairs and established her own alibi.

She was hoping to beat the conspiracy charge, and she probably could. Gower could almost see her, tears in her eyes, telling the jury how she wasn't the least suspicious when her boyfriend asked her questions about her other friend, the Chief Cashier. No, sir, she'd had no idea that Frank was a bank robber, he'd told her he was a businessman. And all the men on the jury, their reason clouded by lust, would believe every word.

Even if she was convicted, she'd most likely get away with two or three years, while the rest of the gang were doing twenty stretches. And when she came out, she'd be in the clear and all the money would be hers. She was nothing but a double-crossing bitch – but then he'd learned long ago never to trust *any* woman!

And yet he found that he didn't really care if she got off scot-free, or if the money was never recovered. He only wanted Mason, and she was helping to get him. For a moment, he felt something towards her that was almost akin to affection.

"And while you were having breakfast, where was Frank? Out with Harry and Tony?"

"Yes, that's right," Linda said.

God, she was handing them to him on a plate. "And do you know where they were?"

"Have you got a cigarette, please?" Linda asked.

The police stenographer dropped his pad and almost fell over himself to extract a cigarette and light it for her. Linda took a long reflective drag, re-crossed her legs, and looked Gower squarely in the face.

"Do you know where they were?" he asked again.

He saw that she was smiling again. It was not one of her sexy leers, it was a wide, amused grin. She reminded him of a magician who is just about to pull a trick that will totally mystify his audience.

"I'm not sure where exactly," she said, "but from what they showed me back at the hotel, I could make a pretty good guess."

Nineteen

As Gower walked down the corridor to Mason's cell, he was thinking about his dream – Mason in chains, the scaffold, the executioner, the escape. When he'd woken up, it had been the escape that had worried him, so he'd examined all the legal loopholes and decided the case was as tightly meshed as it could be. And that had been his mistake. He shouldn't have been thinking about the escape, he should have concentrated on exactly who the executioner was.

Don't get angry, he told himself.

He needed to be calm if he was going to explain to Mason that he had worked it all out – and he wanted to do that very badly.

When the guard opened the door, Mason was sitting on his bunk, smoking a cigarette. He waved it at Gower.

"I'd given up smoking," he said, "but you get so bored in jail, don't you?"

"Mind if I take a seat, Frank?" Gower asked politely.

Mason's face registered surprise. "Please yourself, Mr Gower."

Gower picked up the single institutional chair, and straddled it, arms resting on the back. "I've been running my arse off ever since this case began," Gower said. "There's never really been time to stop and ask myself why you

201

planned such a shitty job, why you made so many obvious mistakes . . ."

"I didn't plan any job, Mr Gower."

"Look Frank," Gower said, "there are no microphones, no hidden cameras, no listeners. I just want to talk the job through with you . . . Oh, all right, for God's sake, I never really had time to stop and ask myself why *somebody* planned such a shitty job."

Mason said nothing.

"For a start, why use Portuguese Pedro? I mean, he's such a bleeding wally, isn't he?"

"Maybe the gang wanted you to think they were Portuguese."

"Yes, that would make sense, especially as Pedro was the only one that spoke. But if they really wanted us to believe they were wogs, why would they leave all that British gear in the getaway car?"

"No eye for detail?" Mason suggested.

"Oh no, Frank, there was a lot of eye for detail on this job. Another point. Why did Arnie the Actor – all right, someone, as yet unknown but calling himself Arthur Blake – why did he hire all three cars for the robbery? And why three cars anyway? You only needed two, one for the actual job and the other for Pedro's getaway, later."

"Beats me," Mason said, "you'd have thought two cars would be enough for anybody."

He was deliberately taunting, but Gower refused to become annoyed – not until he showed Mason how clever he'd been.

"And why did the driver go into the bank?" he continued. "Drivers don't do that, they sit outside, keeping the engine running. If the job needs four men inside – and this one didn't – then you get yourself an extra lad. But whatever happens, the driver stays in the car."

"So I've read," Mason said dryly.

"What would you say, Frank, if I told you that some other bloke was planning to pull a job and that he took on as one of his shotgun men an old lag whose nerve was completely bloody wrecked? That although the planner sent the forward man in on a fake passport, he and the gang used their real names. That the gang had a meal together the night before the robbery and actually drew other people's attention to them by having an argument? What would you say about all that, Frank?"

"That they were complete idiots and a disgrace to the criminal fraternity."

"Or . . . ?"

Mason smiled. "Or they were deliberately going out of their way to get caught."

"Oh, you did your best to get caught, Frank," Gower said. "That's why you sent Linda to hang about near the Banco de Lisboa. So that cashier feller – what's-his-name? – Reis, would notice her and remember all the questions she'd asked him about the bank's business last time she was here. So he'd report it and the police, checking on her, would be led straight to you. I'm not boring you, am I, Frank?"

"No," Mason said. "Carry on."

"And it was important, more important than anything else, that Pedro got caught. Pedro was the fall guy, Pedro was the one who was meant to go to jail."

"Pedro's not a very nice bloke," Mason said mildly, "but still, if he *had* been working a job for me – which he couldn't be because I haven't pulled one – and he'd got caught, I would have seen to it that he got his share of the haul. He'd make more money by going to prison for a while than he's ever seen in his life."

"Pedro was the fall guy," Gower repeated. "Why did Arnie rent the Almera that was Pedro's getaway car? Why didn't Pedro rent the car himself, like he'd rented one the day before?"

"I can see you're bursting to tell me," Mason said.

"Precisely so that even the bloody stupid Portuguese would be able to connect the Almera with the robbery – to make it easier for them to find Pedro. But you didn't expect them to get on to him as quickly as they did – and they wouldn't have if he hadn't crashed the Policia Florestal's roadblock. You didn't know about that, did you?"

"No," Mason admitted. "I haven't had time to nip out and buy a paper today."

"Anyway, because the police got on to him so soon, they were able to work out roughly where he'd hidden the rucksack. And that definitely wasn't planned for. I thought you were worried that we'd found out about the rucksack, but you weren't. You'd have been more worried if we hadn't found out. All you were crapping yourself about was us getting to it too soon."

"Too soon, Mr Gower?"

"While the harbour and airport were still closed. You knew that once we had the robbers and thought we knew where the money was, that tosser Silva would open the airport again and your accomplices could get the money out. That's what Linda was doing on her walk, wasn't it? Checking that things had returned to normal, that they'd had time to get away?"

"Don't know anything about that, Mr Gower," Mason

said. "Didn't even know that Linda had been for a walk. Haven't seen her since we were arrested."

Gower snorted.

"But if it had happened that way," Mason continued, "wouldn't it have been a bit of a Pyrrhic victory?"

"A what?"

"Pyrrhic victory. Named after Pyrrhus, King of Epirus. He fought the Romans and won, but his army got so much shit kicked out of it that he might as well have lost."

"Read a lot, do you, Frank?" Gower asked sarcastically.

"When I get the chance. What I mean about a Pyrrhic victory is, we'd get the money off the island, but we'd end up in jail for twenty years. Money's no good to you in jail."

"That's where you were smart," Gower said. "And I have to admit, Frank, you were very smart. You knew that if you pulled a job on this island you'd get caught, there was no way round it. So you decided *not* to pull a job."

"Say what, Mr Gower?"

"Let's go back to the robbery. Remember – two cars instead of one, driver inside the bank instead of out, only Pedro speaking. I'll tell you why all that happened. Two cars to prevent Pedro from seeing any of the rest of the team without their masks on. That's why the driver had to go inside too – he couldn't very well sit out in the car with a ski-mask over his head. And nobody else spoke so that Pedro wouldn't hear their voices. All that, just so that the poor little plonker wouldn't know who he was working with."

"But surely," Mason said, "he already knew who he was working with, Mr Gower."

"He thought he did, but he didn't. The robbers had the

same build as his friends Frank, Tony and Harry, but they were different people entirely. Who'd you use to play you? Sid Cranshaw? Terry the Bolt? Jack Sodbury?"

Mason didn't speak. Gower hadn't expected him to.

"So, they pull the job, you set yourselves up and are arrested and they make a clean getaway by public bloody transport. Once they're clear, Linda comes up with your alibi. You were on an all-day coach tour round the island when the robbery happened and you can produce thirty reputable witnesses, including, I shouldn't be surprised, a couple of bleeding vicars."

"When did Linda tell you about this?" Mason asked innocently.

"After she'd spoken to her lawyer," Gower replied, walking into the trap. "About half an hour ago."

"And when did she first ask for a lawyer? As soon as she was arrested? Were you deaf with her as well?"

Despite himself, Gower let his head nod slightly.

"So in other words, if you hadn't had wax in your ears, if you'd given her a lawyer right at the start, you'd have known about our alibi while the airport was still closed – while the money was still on the island."

It wasn't true, Gower knew it wasn't. If they had been given lawyers the day before, they'd have come up with another excuse to stall. Still, the throbbing band of pain was back round Gower's chest.

"Don't push your bloody luck, you bastard," he warned.

"Aren't we moving away from the script, Mr Gower, sir?" Mason asked, prodding him further. "Shouldn't you say something like, 'You've been very clever, Frank, but you made one fatal mistake'?"

Gower saw red. He stood up, knocking the metal chair

to one side. Mason smiled slightly, but made no attempt to move.

The Chief Superintendent's hands were bunched into tight fists. He wanted to pulverise Mason, crush his skull, see his blood trickling down the wall. He was already taking a swing when he was hit by an unfamiliar emotion. He had the force of the law behind him no longer, it was just him against Mason – and he was afraid. He let his arms fall impotently to his sides.

"You've got away with it this time," he said. "But you'll pull another job eventually. And when you do, you bastard, I'll be waiting. And God help you when I get my hands on you."

Mason smiled again. "There won't be any more jobs, Mr Gower. I'm going to retire."

Part Three

And Sinker

Thro' all the drama – whether damned or not -
Love gilds the scene, and women guide the plot.
Sheridan: *The School for Scandal*.

Twenty

Elsie heard him turning the key in the lock and opened the door from the inside. She was wearing a pink dressing gown and her hair was in curlers. The expression on her face would have melted down Marble Arch.

"Your Christmas dinner's on the table," she said, "but you're three days late so it's probably cold by now."

No joke, not with Elsie. There it sat, the gravy congealed into a grey hardness, the roast potatoes like rock, the turkey sad and withered.

Mason launched into his prepared story. "Sorry, darlin'," he said. "I ran into Jack Sodbury in Liverpool. We had a few drinks to celebrate, got into a fight and ended up in the nick. The courts only re-opened today. Hundred quid fine."

"Don't make yourself conspicuous, I said," Elsie replied bitterly, hands on hips. "And you get arrested by the police. Well, that buggers up any chance of pulling a job in Liverpool for the next five years, doesn't it? At least, it would if I believed one word you said." She walked over to the telephone. "I think I'll just give Jack a buzz. What's his number?"

"He's not at home," Mason said, as Elsie's finger hovered impatiently over the dial. "He stayed up north. He's on the look-out for likely prospects for his next job."

"Jack Sodbury planning a job," Elsie sneered. "He doesn't

plan jobs, he works for people like you. Do you really think I'm so bloody stupid that I'd believe a story like that? I know what you've been doing, all right."

She stormed out of the lounge. He heard the bedroom door slam behind her.

Mason looked around the room, his gaze finally settling on the coffee table. The *Evening Standard* lay open, an article at the top of the page circled with lipstick – angry bright red lipstick. Even from a distance, Mason could read the headline – Britons Released!

It was datelined Lisbon. There was a picture of Gower looking as if he wanted to hit the photographer, a brief summary of the previous day's report and a statement that the six unnamed Britons arrested on the 23rd had been released, and only the Portuguese was still in detention.

He had been foolish ever to hope that the story would not appear in the papers. Britons abroad were always news, especially at Christmas, when there was a dearth of other stories.

So Elsie knew. But she couldn't have told her father yet, because if she had, Sims' heavies would have been waiting for him at the flat. She would tell him, though, there was no doubt about that.

He had two choices, Mason thought. He could grovel to Elsie now, admit what he had been planning to do, and beg her to take him back. And she probably would – she would like to have that kind of power over him. Or he could go into hiding, and gamble on Ted Sims not finding him before the money arrived. Yet what were the odds of Sims not tracking him down, given the old man's vast net of criminal contacts? Probably about fifty to one, he estimated. He looked at the cold Christmas dinner on the table and pictured spending the rest of his life with Elsie. He would risk the second option, he decided.

Elsie returned, her hair freed from its imprisonment, the dressing gown exchanged for a new lambswool coat.

"Oh, reading about the robbery, are we?" she asked. "When I first saw it, I thought for a minute it might be you, especially when the robbers turned out to be so bloody useless that the police arrested them in no time at all. But then I read that they'd let the robbers go," she added, even more cuttingly, "so I knew it couldn't be you. I said to myself, my Frank hasn't got the brain to get himself out of jail."

"I *was* in jail," Mason said. "In Liverpool. I told you."

"Yes, yes," Elsie replied in a bored, but still vicious tone, "of course you were. You can't fool me, Frank. You picked up some bloody little tart, didn't you?" She checked her hair in the mirror. "I'm off to see Dad now. I may or may not mention your little Christmas fling. It depends how the mood takes me. But if I was you, I wouldn't get too fond of my kneecaps."

She slammed the front door behind her.

She didn't see the obvious truth because she had got so used to underrating him. But Ted didn't. If Ted read about the robbery and pieced it together with the whisper he had heard about Frank working with Pedro, then Mason's kneecaps would definitely go, but only as part of a longer, much more painful process. He wondered where the money was now.

The money was in the carefully crafted hiding place in the *Seaspray* which had been used to transport the shotguns on the voyage out. It was no longer banknotes with funny words on them, but had been changed – by a shady but reliable character in Las Palmas – for good honest British ten-pound notes.

The *Seaspray* itself had just sailed around the southern side of Fuerteventura and was heading for North Africa. They would have to hug the coast all the way home, Nigel had said. December wasn't the best time of the year for sailing in the Atlantic Ocean, and storms had been predicted. It could all take some time.

Susan was really looking forward to New Year's Eve. After years of being stuck at home with her ailing mam and watching the scene on television, she was actually going to be in Trafalgar Square when the chimes of midnight struck. A new year – a new life.

Tony was waiting for her in a pub on the Charing Cross Road. The place was packed with revellers – shouting, telling jokes, breaking into impromptu dances – but Tony did not seem to share the general mood. There was little warmth in his welcoming smile and the kiss he gave her was no more than an apathetic peck. As she talked, he shredded beer mats, breaking off only to glance at his watch.

At nine o'clock, he suddenly stood up. "I've got to make a phone call," he said.

The phone was in the corner, but she could see his face reflected in the mirror behind the bar – troubled at first then spreading into a wide, almost ecstatic, grin.

"Sorry about this," he said, carelessly, when he returned. "I'll have to leave you. Got a bit of business to do."

"Business? On New Year's Eve?"

He shrugged. "That's the way it goes. You can always go on your own, can't you?"

She couldn't, not after all the years of waiting, of dreaming that some day she would have someone special to share the moment with. She was bitterly disappointed, but she didn't let it show. "I'll be all right," she said; though she could tell that he didn't care one way or the other.

When he had left – a spring in his step – she bought a couple of bottles of Babycham and took the tube back to her lodgings.

At five to midnight she was in her sordid little bed-sit, a blanket over her legs to ward off the cold. She switched on the radio.

"The crowd is really thick around Nelson's Column now," the announcer said. "And some of people at the fountain, too impatient to wait for midnight, have already taken a dip."

They sounded happy, all those cheering, shouting people. She opened a bottle of Babycham and poured it into her glass.

"It's a special night, New Year's Eve," the voice on the radio said. "A night to be with the one you love. Are you with the one you love? If you are, then when the clock strikes I want you to give them a big kiss from me."

Susan felt a tear running down her cheek.

"And all of you who's loved ones are far away tonight, I want you to close your eyes and imagine they're right there with you."

She closed her eyes and thought of Frank. Frank was kind and considerate. Frank was like the dad she'd never had. But there was more to him than that. She sensed a different kind of love inside him, a love that was going to waste because he had no one to shower it on. She'd never met his wife, but she didn't think Elsie made him happy. Linda didn't make him happy, either, not happy in the right way. She c—

215

'Dong!' went the chime on the radio.

She wouldn't see Frank again – ever – she resolved.

'Dong!'

She had no right to judge his private life. What did she know?

'Dong!'

But she would finish with Tony – definitely. It wasn't just that she was sure he was seeing other women. He was . . . incomplete. She was glad he had deserted her that night; he wasn't special enough to share a New Year with.

She realised she'd never have thought that before she met Frank.

It was a bit like seeing the sea. When she'd been a kid, she'd thought Accrington was the whole world, and she'd been happy with it – at least, not too miserable. Then her mam, by saving and scraping, had managed to get enough money together for a day-trip to Blackpool. And once she'd splashed her feet in the water and run along the sands, her hometown had never looked quite the same again.

That was what Frank had done to the way she saw people. She'd noticed something special about him the first time they'd met – when he hadn't wanted her to go with them to Madeira. But it hadn't been until after the police released them that she'd really come to appreciate how marvellous he was.

They'd gone to a nightclub to celebrate. Everyone had been almost hysterically happy. Except her. She'd felt cheapened, humiliated, by all the things that horrible policeman had said to her. And the worst thing was, he'd been right. She'd thought she might learn to love Tony, but it simply hadn't happened. Yet she'd come on holiday with him, shared his bed. So what was she, after all, but 'Tony's whore'?

Tony had been the life and soul of the party, knocking back drinks like water, dancing with Linda and Mrs Snell. He'd asked her to dance and when she'd refused he hadn't even noticed how low she felt. But Frank had.

"Got the blues, darlin'? You need a breath of fresh air. Let's go for a walk."

"No," she'd protested. "It's not right. It's your night, Mr Mason."

"This doesn't matter," gesturing around at the glamorous decor, "none of it."

He'd taken her by the arm and walked her along the promenade. He hadn't spoken and neither had she. She'd heard the insects in the grass and felt the sea breeze blowing through her hair, and she'd started to feel better.

"I'll see you back to your room," he'd said.

He'd done more than that. He'd entered the room with her, turned his back while she undressed, and stayed with her until she fell asleep . . .

She realised that the clock had long since stopped chiming and that her Babycham had gone flat.

"I won't see him again," she said, squaring her jaw. "I won't, I won't!"

Two things were bothering Ted Sims as he sat warming his feet before the fire that cold morning in early January. The first was his one and only child – Elsie. She had visited him nearly every day since Christmas, and while he was flattered by her attention he couldn't help being suspicious. She was asking a lot of questions, too – and that wasn't like her.

'Read anything interesting in the papers today, Daddy?'

'Got something on your mind, Daddy?'

Which was strange, because there *was* something on his mind – quite apart from her behaviour. Ever since his talk with his son-in-law some months earlier – when he'd mentioned the rumours that Mason was planning a job – he'd had an uneasy feeling that somehow Frank had conned him. And the whispers were still going on: Mason had got a team together, Mason was pulling a job soon, Mason was pulling a job abroad.

So he'd been disturbed when he read about the robbery in Madeira. Frank and Elsie had been there for their holidays – and maybe Frank really was working with Pedro.

He'd told himself that it was always like that with 'abroad': if you had a cousin living in Australia and you read about a bush fire, you were sure – even if he lived in Melbourne and hated the bloody outback – that he was one of the victims. But the nagging doubt wouldn't go away. If only the papers had given some bloody names.

"Seen Portuguese Pedro recently?" he asked the short broad heavy who served as his butler-minder.

"Can't say I have, Mr Sims."

"See if you can round him up for me."

The heavy nodded.

"And another thing . . . I want the names of the fellers behind this Madeiran job. Is Toad Gower still as bloody lily-white as he was, or is he accepting contributions to his retirement fund these days?"

"He's the same as ever. Doesn't like villains, Mr Sims."

"So who can we get at?"

The heavy shook his head doubtfully. "Difficult since the last clean up. Couple of Chief Inspectors, a few DIs."

"Get on to them. See if they can come up with something."

"Right away, Mr Sims."

A cruiser like the *Seaspray* can weather most storms by reefing the sails and heading straight into the wind, but it is a tiring process to repeat too often. Besides, even though the crew were shaping up well they were still inexperienced, and Nigel thought it wiser to put into port whenever the meteorological forecast was too threatening.

So they made steady progress up the coast of Morocco, stopping off at Agadir to wait out one storm and Rabat to let another pass. But there was no way of avoiding the one that hit them unexpectedly off the coast of Portugal, and they were forced to put in to Oporto for essential maintenance.

By the time Ted Sims started to get ideas about the Madeiran job, they were crossing the Bay of Biscay and hoping to Christ that the weather had no more surprises in store for them.

It had taken a great deal of self-discipline and three Babychams before Susan had been able to pluck up the courage to ring Tony's doorbell a week after that terrible New Year's Eve, and when he didn't answer she was tempted just to write a note and go home. Then she remembered what her mam used to say.

'If you're so ashamed to say it that you have to do it by letter, then you shouldn't be sayin' it at all.'

Mam was right. She had nothing to be ashamed of, she was just going to tell Tony that it was all over between them. She reached into her plastic handbag, took out the key that Tony had given her, and unlocked the door.

Once she was in the flat, the drink started to affect her. Not that she felt dizzy or sick, just very, very tired, as if she could sink down into the floor and just keep on sinking. She didn't know when Tony would be home, and she was too exhausted to sit in the armchair. She went into the bedroom and lay down, intending just to rest her eyes for a while, and then . . .

She was awoken abruptly by the front door being slammed closed. She got off the bed, searched drowsily for her shoes, and was just about to enter the living room when she heard a female voice saying her name.

"Have you seen Susan since you dumped her on New Year's Eve?" Linda asked.

Tony, on the point of opening the cocktail cabinet, suddenly tensed up. "No, I haven't," he said guiltily.

He opened the whisky bottle, poured himself a shot, and knocked it straight back. He was drinking too much these days, Linda thought, and she suspected that if she hadn't been with him he'd have taken it straight from the bottle.

"Have you slept with her since we got back from Madeira?"

"I don't want to. I can't. I'd just be thinking of you."

"And don't you know that I'm only thinking of you when I'm with Frank?" Linda asked. "But we have to do it, just for a little while longer, so they don't get suspicious."

Tony poured himself another drink. He was getting very difficult to handle. She had seduced him both mentally and physically, and like an ex-virgin the morning after, he was subject to regrets.

Frank had been good to him, he told her. Why didn't they treat him fairly? Couldn't they just take their share of the money and go away? They would still have each other.

She couldn't tell him the truth, which was that he wasn't enough for her – wasn't even the main thing she wanted. It was the money that really mattered, and he was just a pleasant little bonus like a free corkscrew with a good bottle of wine. She knew that she could keep control of him and his scruples only by maintaining his addiction to her body. And right now it was time to give him a fix.

"Forget about Susan, forget about Frank," she said. "Let's do it! Let's do it here and now."

And as she spoke, she began slowly to unbutton her blouse. Tony stood gaping, as he always did. She opened her blouse slightly, giving him a glimpse of her marvellous, wonderful breasts, and then slowly, sensuously, peeled it off. She walked over to him, rubbing herself against his chest as she undid his trousers and slid them down to his ankles.

"Lie down," she said huskily.

He lowered himself on to the living-room carpet.

She stood over him so that he was looking up at her; up at her legs, disproportionate from that angle but even more beautiful because of it; up at her breasts, firm and promising; up at her wide generous mouth. Slowly she slipped out of her skirt, then let her panties fall to the floor.

"We're going to have the best of times," she said, lowering herself on to him.

He groaned as she started to move, slowly, rhythmically, teasing.

"It will always be like this," she said, "always this wonderful. We'll never get bored with it, will we? Never!"

"No," Tony moaned. "No."

"We can have a wonderful time, Tony, with all that money. All of it."

"Yes, yes!"

She had achieved her aim, at least for a little while. She surrendered to sensation, immersing herself in the sex as deeply as Tony. Neither of them heard the soft footfalls on the carpet or the soft click of the front door closing.

*   *   *

221

"I had to tell you, Frank, I had to." Susan was crying as she spoke, not for herself but for Mason, who was sitting in an easy chair, his hands clutching the arms, like a man half-dead.

He was already under pressure – waiting for the moment Elsie told her father about his disappearance over Christmas and Sims would put two and two together and send his men after him. And now this. He felt a pain far beyond tears. He had lost Linda. That hurt, but deep down he was not really surprised. He had never been able to handle women. Far worse was that Tony, the son he had never been allowed to have, was plotting behind his back. And betraying not just him, but everybody who had been involved in the operation. Even poor old Pedro wouldn't get his severance pay if Linda and Tony's plan – whatever it was – worked out.

"You're terribly upset, Frank, I can see you are," Susan said softly.

She walked over to him, placed one hand on his shoulder and began stroking his hair. "There, there," she said, just as she had so many times to her sick mam. "It seems bad now, but it will get better."

As she stroked, he felt the tension drain out of him, as it had done at the outdoor iron kiosk in Madeira. He turned and faced her, and before he knew what was happening, he was holding her in his arms, kissing her.

Ted Sims' usually reliable sources were drawing a complete blank.

'I tried to get Toady Gower to talk about it, but he's keeping very quiet about this particular case,' one DCI told Ted's minder.

'It's almost like he was embarrassed by what happened on Madeira. So no names. Sorry,' said another, regretfully

222

turning down the envelope of money for services he was unable to render.

Which left Ted Sims with nothing more than a few vague whispers and his nagging doubt. He would tackle Frank about it directly, he decided, but first he would talk to Elsie.

He brought it up the next morning. They were in his study, he sitting at his desk with the morning papers, she arranging the large bunch of lilies she had brought for him.

"When did Frank get back from Liverpool?" he wondered aloud.

"Why do you ask, Daddy?"

"Well, you remember when you wanted me to sniff around and see if Frank was planning to pull a job he'd not told you about?"

"Yes."

"I think he might already have pulled it. The bank job in Madeira over Christmas."

Elsie took a pair of sharp scissors and neatly snipped the ends off a number of stems. Then she placed the flowers in a Chinese vase and fussed with their composition.

"Elsie?"

"I'm thinking about it, Daddy. No, not Frank. He's too thick to pull a job on his own in England, let alone abroad."

Her father shook his head. "You don't give him enough credit. I've always said that."

Elsie frowned. "Maybe you're right," she admitted. "When was the job?"

"The twenty-third."

"Hmm, Frank was away then. I saw him catch the train

to Liverpool on the nineteenth, but I suppose that would have given him plenty of time to get to Madeira. And I rang Tony several times over the next few days – and he was never in."

"If it was him . . ." Sims growled.

"I thought I'd read that they'd caught the robbers."

"They did, but they had to let them go again on Christmas Eve."

Elsie laughed lightly. "Oh well, it couldn't have been Frank. He was back home again by then."

Twenty-One

"It's tonight," Mason said over the phone.

"Tonight?" Tony replied. "But he wasn't supposed to arrive for another couple of . . ."

"Tonight. He's made better time than he expected, and the weather report's good. I'll pick you up at five."

The line went dead.

Had there been a cold edge to Frank's voice? Tony wondered. Hadn't he sounded more as if he was talking to a casual acquaintance rather than to a close friend?

"But then I'm *not* a close friend, am I?" he whispered. "I'm a traitor, a back-stabber."

If only he could convince himself that Frank would do the same to him if their situations were reversed. But he knew Frank would never let him down – Frank would never let anybody down.

He walked into the bathroom and flicked the switch over the mirror. The lights picked out his face as clearly as if he were on the stage – or under an interrogator's lamp.

"I am double-crossing Frank," he said to his reflection. "I am double-crossing Frank."

The image which mouthed the words silently in time with him was the one he was accustomed to seeing – clear eyes, healthy, glowing skin, the face of a man who looked less

225

than his years. "So why do I feel so rotten inside?" he asked his reflected self.

He returned to the living room and surveyed it as if were new to him – the comfortable sofa, the sheepskin rug, his beloved CD collection. After that night's work, he could say goodbye to it all.

There was no point in putting it off any longer. He picked up the phone and dialled a familiar number.

"It's tonight," he said, echoing Mason's words. "Will you be ready?"

He was half-hoping that she would say no.

"I'll be ready," Linda said. "And by tomorrow night we'll be in Rio. Remember the picture of the hotel room, Tony? It's got a big, big bed."

When he hung up, he was disgusted to discover that he had an erection.

Fishing boats chugged slowly into the harbour, scores of seagulls following in their wake. In front of the stone houses, old women dressed in black sat on stunted chairs, knitting and watching their little world go by.

The place had almost a picture-postcard prettiness about it, Nigel thought. When the job was over, he'd buy himself another boat and spend a lot of his time moored in places like this.

The harbour master, his pipe clenched between toothless gums, a tattered chart under his arm, was walking along the quay. He stopped by the side of the *Seaspray* and glanced down at the cast-off bowlines.

"You are leaving, monsieur?" he asked.

"Yes."

"I think it might perhaps be wiser to delay your trip,"

the old man said, pointing up at the cumulonimbus clouds which hung heavily in the sky. "There will be a storm, of that there is no doubt. And there are predictions of a gale, perhaps a force eight or nine."

"We're only going a little up the coast," Nigel said, "as far as Boulogne."

The harbour master stroked his bushy white beard thoughtfully. "Even so, Monsieur," he said, "it might be prudent to wait."

"We'll be there before the bad weather really sets in."

The old man gave one of those shrugs that the French have patented. "It is your business, monsieur. Well, *bon voyage.*"

He walked away, his wellingtons squeaking on the cobblestones.

Nigel turned to Jack Sodbury. "You can release the slip-lines now," he said in English.

"What was the old feller wittering on about, Skipper?" Jack asked.

"Oh, he was just asking me where we were going. I didn't tell him the truth, of course."

"He looked like he was warning you about bad weather when he pointed up the clouds."

"Quite the contrary. He was telling me they should clear up in an hour or so – but I knew that already." He slapped Sodbury on the shoulder. "You're getting quite good at handling a boat, Jack, old chap, but you've got a lot learn about reading the weather." He glanced at his watch. "And since we're due to meet Frank in a few hours, we'll set sail now. That is, if we have your permission, Mr Sodbury?"

The other man grinned and gave a mock salute. "Aye, aye, sir."

The lines were pulled, and the boat began to manoeuvre its way out of its mooring.

There was almost a full moon, but the black clouds drifting heavily across the sky obscured it for most of the time.

Mason slowed the Land-rover to a halt. "This is the place," he said.

They were the first words he had spoken since the journey began. He had not trusted himself to say anything to the man who was about to betray him. Even now, he found it hard to deliver this simple phrase without a trace of the hurt and bitterness he felt seeping into it.

Tony just nodded. If he had found Mason's silence strange, he had not commented on it. He got out of the vehicle and walked a few yards up the road. In the head-lights, Mason could see him neatly cutting through the barbed-wire fence. When he had finished, Mason edged the Land-rover through the gap.

Tony removed the roll of wire from the back of the vehicle and began to repair the fence. Even on a country lane in the middle of the night, it was possible that a passing motorist would notice a damaged fence and stop to investigate. True, it was only a *slim* possibility, but it was not worth taking even the slightest chance at this crucial stage of the operation.

Mason drove slowly down the sloping field. Cows, settled down for the night, shifted uneasily but did not move. At the far fence, Mason stopped and got out. He could still see the road from where he was, but the angle was such that the lights of passing cars would not pick out the shape of the Land-rover. He had taken that into consideration when selecting the spot.

I took everything into consideration, he thought, apart from the fact that I couldn't trust the man I'd have given my life for.

He could hear the roar of the sea, and the wind as it whistled through the telephone wires. Branches on a nearby tree bent and creaked. He wondered why Nigel hadn't waited for better weather. Maybe he just wanted to get it over with.

"That's all I want," he said softly to himself, "to get it over with."

Tony appeared out of the darkness. Together, they unstrapped the small boat from the roof rack and manhandled it down to the sea.

It had been Frank's idea to use the boat. "The Customs and Excise might decide to carry out a random check on the *Seaspray* the moment it lands," he'd told his team, "and if they do, you're going to have a hard time explaining all that money away. So the safest thing to do is unload it before you reach Brighton Marina."

Yes, that had only seemed like sense at the time, but *at the time*, he hadn't known what he knew now.

The two men returned to the vehicle for the outboard motor and fixed it to the craft. And then there was nothing to do but wait for Nigel's signal.

Mason watched Tony walking up and down, hugging himself occasionally. Was he nervous, or just cold?

Susan, with tears in her eyes, had begged Mason not to do this – implored him not to put himself in a position where he was alone with Tony.

'I have to,' he'd told her.

'Why, when you know he's going to double-cross you?'

'Because I have to be sure he'd really go through with it. And if I don't give him the chance, I'll never know.'

But he will go through with it, Mason thought to himself as he stood on the dark windswept beach, studying Tony's body language. Linda's got him in her grip, and he'll do whatever she asks him to.

When would he make his play? And what form would that play take? Would he drive away while his unsuspecting boss was ordering two teas-to-go from a transport cafe? Or would he sneak up behind Mason and hit him on the head? Without Susan's warning, either would have been easy. Even with the warning, he might still pull it off. Yet even now, Mason couldn't bring himself to deny the man he loved almost as a son the chance to prove he was worthy of that love.

Jack Sodbury shone his torch down on the water and saw, as he'd expected, that it was rough. He edged his way carefully round to the cockpit where Nigel Monk was standing confidently at the tiller.

"It's getting choppy, Skipper," Sodbury shouted. "Wind-speed must be up to twenty-five knots by now."

"Nonsense," Nigel replied. "Can't be more than eighteen. Ideal cruising wind. And for God's sake keep that torch out of my eyes. D'you want to impair my night vision?"

He was wrong about the windspeed, Sodbury thought. And not only that, but he must *know* he was wrong from the amount of spray that been hitting the deck for the last twenty minutes. "I think we should heave-to and ride it out, Skipper," he said.

"You want to take over the tiller?" Nigel demanded.

In that weather? A novice like him? Maybe in the daytime, but not at night when sailing even in perfect conditions was difficult enough. "No, I don't," Sodbury said. "But I—"

"So I'm still Captain, am I?" Nigel interrupted. "In that case, you'll obey orders. I want the mainsail double-reefed

and the hatches battened down. And I want all crew on deck
– in harnesses. Get to it."

Sodbury felt angry and impotent. However crazy the Skipper's instructions seemed, they'd be lost without him, so there
was no choice but to do what he said. But harnesses – for what
he claimed was only an eighteen-knot wind? And if he wanted
the hatches closed he was expecting it to get worse.

And get worse it did. The boat rocked and swayed, waves
started to break over the hull, the bilge had to be pumped out
every few minutes.

"It's a gale," Jack Sodbury thought, panicking. He gazed
into the black night that engulfed the tiny boat. "It's a gale,
and we're all going to die."

He edged his way into the cockpit. Water slopped around
at his feet. "Heave-to!" he screamed above the noise of the
wind. "Bloody heave-to!"

"We're almost there," Nigel shouted back.

"We're not almost bleeding anywhere!"

And then, in the distance, Sodbury saw three or four
tiny twinkling lights that could be shining only from the
English coast.

It was tough dragging the small boat to the edge of the
water, and Linda cursed Tony every inch of the way for not
being there to help her. It would have been a simple matter
to knock Frank out when he wasn't looking – it might have
been an even better idea to finish him off, then there would
never have been any danger of his finding them. But Tony
had insisted that it be done this way, him keeping Frank
busy, her with a second craft two miles further down the
coast making the real pick-up.

She watched the waves breaking, and shuddered. Nigel

would come as close in as he could, but she would still have to go out in that little boat through the rough sea. She knelt down and put her hand in the water. It was like ice.

She shouldn't have to do this! Tony should be with her. It should be Tony who risked the boat trip to collect the money. Maybe he didn't deserve to share it with her after all. Maybe once she'd used him to get rid of Nigel, she'd take off on her own and have all that lovely money all to herself.

The shortwave radio by her side hissed and crackled.

"*Seaspray* to Linda. *Seaspray* to Linda. Are you receiving me? Over."

She clicked the switch to transmit. "Not very clearly, but I can hear you. Over."

"Coming in. Expect to be off-shore from you within forty-five, repeat forty-five minutes. Start signalling after thirty. Over and out."

"Are you sure you can . . ." Linda began, but Nigel had already signed off.

She lit a cigarette and inhaled greedily. Icy gusts of wind cut into her face. Why couldn't Nigel have got there earlier, to save all this waiting around?

She heard a noise behind her. At first she thought it was only the sound of a tin can being blown along the beach, but then she realised that it was too regular for that. Footsteps crunching on the shingle! She turned her head, and could just make the figures out in what pale moonlight the clouds had allowed to filter through. Two of them, heading towards her. She stubbed her cigarette and squatted down by the boat.

She wondered for a second if they were strollers, but they couldn't be. There was only one group of people who would turn out on a filthy night like this – policemen! What could she say, how could she explain her presence by the boat?

The Paradise Job

She couldn't, of course. She would have no choice but to save herself by turning the others in.

They had started out as nothing more than vague shapes, their edges blurring into the darkness, but as they got closer, their forms became more distinct. Both were men, both tall, although one was bulky and the other slim. She felt her heart sink as they approached. The slim one reached her first.

"I couldn't do it, Linda," he said apologetically. "I couldn't let Frank down."

So after all her efforts, all her scheming, she had failed. Her grip on Tony was weaker than Mason's. She was angry with herself. And furious, with both her lovers. She sprang to her feet.

"You bloody idiot, Tony," she screamed, slapping him as hard as she could across his face.

He took the blow unflinchingly – as if he had deserved it. She lifted back her hand to strike him again.

"Leave him alone, Linda," Frank said, in a tone that brooked no refusal.

They stood on the beach, looking at each other, yet barely able to distinguish their faces, while around them the waves crashed and the wind whistled.

"So what do we do now?" Linda asked bitterly.

"Now," Mason said, "we wait for Nigel to appear. We play out the end of the double-cross."

He turned to Tony. "Will the rest of the crew still be with him on the boat, by the way?"

"No," Tony replied. "That's all been taken care of."

Twenty-Two

"When I was at school," Nigel Monk said, one hand resting on the tiller, the other holding a Luger, "I was in the Officer Training Corps. And I was a crack shot. I could kill you easily – and I will do if I have to."

It was one of those speeches that sophisticated secret agents make in thrillers, and it sounded polished and rehearsed – which it had been. It was a pity that it was wasted on the three men at whom he was pointing the gun – the howling wind ensured that they only caught one word in three. 'When . . . at . . . was . . . Officer . . . and . . .' But at least they got the general message.

Jack Sodbury started to advance slowly towards him. Nigel waited until he was close enough to talk but not so near that he could try any heroics.

"That's far enough!" he ordered, and Sodbury stopped immediately.

It was funny, Nigel thought, how on land he was so weak and indecisive, but once on a boat he became masterful.

"We worked for that bleeding money," Sodbury said. "We did the robbery, we took the risks. You're not going to take it off us now."

"Just watch me," Nigel said.

"You can't keep your eye on all three of us until we get

to Brighton Marina. You'll drop your guard and then we'll bloody have you."

"No you won't, because you're not going to Brighton. You get off here." He made a rapid gesture with the barrel of his gun towards the tender.

"You can't send us off in that," Sodbury shouted. "It's certain death."

"We're only about two hundred yards from the shore," Nigel replied. "You should make it safely enough. On the other hand, if you don't do as I say, I'll pull the trigger and that *is* certain death."

Sodbury tried once more. "You'll never handle the boat alone, not in this weather. You know you won't."

"I'll worry about that," Nigel replied. "You get into the tender. Now!"

The tender bobbed up and down in the water. Sodbury lowered himself into it and sat on the central thwart, gripping the side for support. With his free hand he slotted in one oar and then the other. Only when they were firmly in place did he signal that the other two men should join him. Slowly, carefully they climbed down. When they were settled and the tender was as stable as it was ever going to be, Sodbury pushed it away from the *Seaspray*.

The small craft was pitching dangerously. Sodbury began to row, pulling heavily on the starboard side to compensate for the current. Despite the cold, despite the waves which soaked him in the first ten seconds, he was sweating. Already his muscles ached. It was only a short distance to the shore, but the effort it would take to get there would be tremendous.

Behind him, the wind carried the sound of the *Seaspray*'s engine starting up.

"I hope for your sake you drown, you bastard," Sodbury muttered through gritted teeth. "Because that's nothing to what's going to happen to you if I ever get my hands on you."

Waves exploded against the bow of the boat, raising it out of the water, threatening to tip them into the black murky sea. Sodbury's muscles felt as if they were on fire.

It was half an hour before the three men, cold, wet and totally penniless, dragged themselves on to the shore.

The black skeletal trees in front of the moon were shaking, the waves were getting higher and higher – and Nigel was late. Fifteen minutes earlier it would have been possible to use the small boat, Mason thought, but not any longer. He wasn't prepared to risk anybody's life just for the money.

The shortwave receiver crackled, harsh bursts of static, then faintly, distortedly a voice came through.

"Linda, Linda, can you hear me?"

Linda looked across at Mason. He had won, he was in charge now, and she was awaiting his instructions.

"Answer it, for Christ's sake," he said.

Linda clicked the button. "Yes, I'm here. Over."

"Can't control the boat any more. She's shipping water. I . . . I think she's going to capsize."

"Well, what do you expect me to do?" Linda asked.

"Get help . . . Call the coast guard . . . anything. I'm frightened, Linda. I don't want to die. I . . ."

There was a final crackle and the radio went dead. Linda dropped it on to the beach and its plastic case shattered.

"Shit!" she said. "Shit, shit, shit! Now none of us get the money."

Mason took out his mobile phone, then threw it angrily on to the shingles when he realised there was no coverage.

He started to run up the beach, his feet slipping on smooth stones. "I'm going to look for a phone box," he called back to Tony, over his shoulder.

The storm built up, relentlessly climbing the Beaufort Scale. The wind had risen to forty-five knots, and fifty-foot waves smashed into the side of HMS *Taunton Castle*, three miles off the shore.

Both the Captain and the First Officer were on the bridge when a message came through from the Watch that he had spotted navigation lights on the starboard bow, and that whatever the vessel was, it was moving bloody fast.

The First Officer looked out of the window and established visual contact himself. The lights were like fireflies, bobbing up and down in the darkness. No mast lights, so it must be a fairly small craft. There was the white of the stern light and the red of the port-side one. Why the hell wasn't there a green starboard light? Either the boat was sailing parallel to them but in the opposite direction or . . . But it couldn't be – because it was getting nearer all the time.

"Must be on its side, sir," he said to the Captain. "Carried by the current and heading straight for us!"

As the Captain ordered evasive action, the First Officer watched the lights getting closer and closer, until he could see the dim shape of the boat between them.

The bump against the side of the ship could have been just another wave – but it wasn't. It was the impact of a twenty-seven-foot Vancouver cruiser battering against a thick metal hull. In the unfair contest the HMS *Taunton Castle* was virtually unmarked, but the *Seaspray* disintegrated.

*   *   *

237

Linda finished her cigarette and threw it down on to the shingle. "Well I'm off," she said to Tony. "Do you want a lift?"

"Off?"

"There's nothing I can do here, is there? I mean, if Nigel's not dead already, he's as good as, isn't he? So do you want that lift or not?"

"No," Tony said. "No, I don't. I'd rather crawl back on my hands and knees than take a lift from you."

Both the words and the tone stung her. "Please your bloody self, then," she said.

It was the second time she had sworn in as many minutes – but after all, she had been provoked.

The wet seemed to have seeped right through to her bones, and it was a relief to reach the rented car. When she switched on the heater, it blew only cold air at her, but it would soon warm up as she drove along. She put the vehicle into first gear and pulled off.

The country lane twisted and turned, and even though she was an excellent driver the going was slow. The wipers clicked back and forth monotonously, clearing the windscreen of rain. She flicked on the radio.

"Hello all you night owls out there," the DJ said with red-eyed cheerfulness. "You're listening to the Golden Oldie show. The year is 1970, the year Edward Heath – remember him? – became Prime Minister and this is Freda Payne with 'Band of Gold'."

The heater had warmed up her feet and she was beginning to feel a little better, but it would be nice to get home and have a long hot bath. She hit the main road to London and increased her speed.

She listened to the singer lament that all she had left of

her marriage was her wedding ring. "Well, I've done better than that," she thought cheerfully.

There was the flat for a start. And Nigel's life insurance – maybe they'd pay more because he died in an accident.

The road was clear and she pressed her foot down to the floor. She was making good time now.

"1979. Woody Allen makes Manhattan and Gloria Gaynor is number one in the charts, telling us that *she* doesn't need a man to survive."

And neither do I, Linda thought.

She had lost Tony, but he had never been anything but the icing on the cake. There would be no more gangsters for her; the next man would be rich, and old – and very easy to please.

She took the bend slightly wide, but would still have been fine if she hadn't hit the patch of loose chippings. The tyres shrieked and she went into a skid. She braked violently, took her foot off immediately and pulled hard on the wheel, setting the car back on a true course. It was only then that she saw the lorry.

It was a little further up the road, its back lights flashing continuously. There was no time to stop. As the wheels of Linda's car crunched over the red warning triangle, she wrenched at the steering with all her might.

She almost made it. Only the back bumper touched the lorry, and it was no more than a glancing blow. But at that speed it was enough. The car shot across the road, spinning out of control. Right in front of the juggernaut approaching from the other direction.

Twenty-Three

"Mind the steps, they'll be slippery after all that rain," the middle-aged coastguard said, placing his own foot carefully on a metal rung.

Mason looked up. Apart from a few cotton-wool clouds which were drifting towards the early morning sun, the sky was completely clear. It was hard to believe that only a few hours earlier nature could have been so savage and unrelenting.

"Of course, we don't know for sure that it was your friend's cruiser which was involved in the collision – although I must admit we've had no reports of any other boats being out at sea last night."

The coastguard was a decent bloke, Mason thought, a kind bloke trying to be as tactful as possible in a difficult situation.

They reached the beach. "If there is any wreckage," the coastguard said, "it should have been washed up somewhere along this stretch."

The storm had spewed all kinds of objects on to the beach: oil drums, soggy and virtually unrecognisable cigarette packets, plastic bottles. The coastguard bent down, and picked something up. He held out the object for Mason's inspection. It was a splintered piece of wood, perhaps two feet long, by five or six inches broad, but unlike most of the surrounding driftwood it was smooth and highly lacquered.

"It's from a boat, all right," the coastguard continued. "Of course, we don't know it came from the *Seaspray*. Could have been in the sea a while. Although," he continued, examining the edge, "I have to say that this splintering looks fairly recent."

It was the *Seaspray* all right, Mason knew it was. Nigel had been out in a storm on a boat too big to be handled by one man. If there'd been a second tender, he might have had a chance – Jack Sodbury and co. had made it, Tony had picked them up a few miles down the coast. But there hadn't been another tender, and besides, by the time Linda picked up his second message, it was already too late – the weather had turned so foul that even a lifeboat crew would have hesitated before putting to sea.

They walked further along the beach. They found no more of the *Seaspray*, but lying next to an old tyre the coastguard discovered a wad of mushy brown paper, tied up with an elastic band.

"That's money," he said. "Tenners." He picked up the soggy bundle. "There must be several hundred quid here. Do you think it belonged to your friend?"

"Yes," Mason said.

"Bloody hell! It was a lot to be carrying around, wasn't it?"

It was only a tiny portion of the whole, Mason thought. But that, and a few other bundles which would be picked up by lucky beachcombers, was all that was left. The rest, the reward for his planning, the compensation for all the strain he had been through, was at the bottom of the sea – with poor bloody Nigel.

"Did he always have this much on him?" the coastguard asked.

"Oh, yes," Mason replied. "He liked to be prepared for emergencies."

The hall was completely bare; the table, the mirror, the carpets – everything – had gone. There was nothing left in the living room either, except for one trunk on which Elsie was sitting. Well, at least she'd had the guts to wait and tell him to his face, Mason thought.

"So this is it," he said.

"This is it," Elsie agreed. "You can't really blame me, can you? You'd have done the same if you'd had the chance. I heard about Nigel Monk's boat sinking on the radio. I take it that was where you had the money stashed from the Madeiran job." She laughed at his startled expression. "Did you really think you could hide it from me for ever?"

He shook his head. No, not really. He had always known deep down that Elsie would get the better of him in the end.

"How long have you known?" he asked.

"Since well before Christmas."

Seeing him off at Euston Station, cooking his Christmas dinner and leaving it on the table – all that had been part of a game, Elsie showing for the final time that she would always be one step ahead.

"Where's the furniture?" he asked. "Gone to auction?"

Elsie nodded. "I've sold the lease on the flat, too. And the Alfa. The safe-deposit box is still there, but it's empty."

"You can't leave me with nothing," he said.

"Oh, but I can, Frank. And I will. If I'm going to put a few thousand miles between me and my nice Catholic Daddy, I'll need all the cash I can lay my hands on."

"If the Madeiran job had come off," Mason said, "I wouldn't have left you destitute. I was going to send you half my share."

Elsie laughed again. "I believe you, Frank. You always were a mug. But I want it all . . . and you're going to let me take it."

"No!"

"Yes." She reached into her handbag, pulled out a brown envelope and handed it to him. "Have a look at those," she said.

Mason opened the envelope and took out a number of glossy black and white photographs. They were taken at night, the only illumination provided by a streetlight, but they were clear enough.

They all focused on a door. Mason recognised it as the entrance to the bed-sit in Matlock Road. In each photograph, there was a different person standing there: Mason himself, Linda, Tony, Portuguese Pedro, Harry Snell, Jack Sodbury, Arnie the Actor, the rest of the gang.

"All Toad Gower needs to pin this job on you is something to tie you in with everybody else," Elsie said. "These pictures would just about do it, don't you think? You'd end up with a long stretch, and you couldn't stand that, could you, Frank? And you couldn't even ask for it to be taken into consideration that you'd returned the money," she chuckled, "because it's all in the Bank of Dogger."

Mason wasn't laughing. He thought back to a visit he'd made months earlier; a dingy flat where the only things of any value were laid out on the coffee table – cameras!

"Nigel," he said.

"Nigel," Elsie agreed. "He seems to have been better at taking pictures than he was at sailing boats. I caught him hiding in a car, watching one of your meetings. Scared him shitless. He'd been taking photographs for weeks. For insurance, I should think, or maybe he was going to try his arm at a spot of blackmail. I didn't ask, I just offered him a deal."

"A deal?"

"If he handed the photographs over to me, I wouldn't tell you that he'd taken them. I can't say he was very gracious about it, but he agreed anyway. You can keep those as a souvenir, Frank. I've got lots of other copies."

Mason sighed. "You win, Elsie," he said.

His wife smiled triumphantly back at him. "Course I bloody do," she crowed.

Epilogue

The couple walking along the Grand Union Canal that pleasant summer afternoon got more than a passing glance from several people. It was not the fact that he was much older than her which drew their attention. Nor was it because he looked so big and powerful and she, despite her obvious pregnancy, so fragile and innocent. What really made them special was that they were so totally absorbed in one another that they hardly seemed aware of the fact that there was a world beyond their two selves.

"Are you sure this walk isn't too much for you?" Frank asked, a concerned edge to his voice.

Susan laughed. "Back home in Lancashire, women used to work in the mills almost up to the moment they gave birth."

"They used to go down coal mines as well," Frank said, "but you and our baby are going to have a better life than that."

They reached Little Venice. "Let's go for a drink," he suggested, pointing across at the tables outside a riverside pub.

"Can we afford it?" Susan asked.

Frank jiggled the coins in his pocket. "Oh, I think so," he said carelessly. "Just about, anyway."

245

They sat under an umbrella, sipping their drinks and watching the swans. "Don't worry your head about money," Frank said. "By the time the baby's born, we'll be rolling in it."

"Really?" Susan said sceptically.

"Well, we'll have enough to be comfortable anyway," Frank conceded. He reached into his shirt pocket and pulled out a business card. "What do you think of that?"

Susan ran her finger over the embossed letters. "The Mason Security Company, plc. Frank Mason, Managing Director," she read aloud.

Frank looked slightly embarrassed. "You've got to be a bit flash when you're in business," he said, almost apologetically.

"How are Jack Sodbury and the rest of them settling into the job?" Susan asked.

"They're taking to it like ducks to water," Frank told her. "After all, it only means standing on the other side of the counter for a change, doesn't it?"

Susan narrowed her eyes as if she were trying to read his mind. "I still haven't worked out whether you started the firm for yourself – or for them," she said.

"I suppose it was a bit of both," Frank replied. "I felt I had to do something for them after the Madeira job fell through." He coughed, awkwardly. "And speaking of the lads, I hope you don't mind, but I've asked Tony to meet us here."

"So you didn't just come here on a whim. It was all planned!" Susan said accusingly.

"That's right," he confessed.

"But *why*, Frank?"

He shrugged. "You can't go through life bearing grudges. Tony had his chance to double-cross me, and he didn't take it. It's time to forgive him. And I'd like *you* to forgive him, as well."

Susan shook her head in mock despair. "Are you *ever* going to stop trying to make things right for everybody else, Frank?"

"Probably not," he answered

Tony appeared on the tow path, stood there for a second, and then made his way hesitantly towards their table. "How are you, Susan?" he asked. "It's got to be said, you're looking great. Pregnancy suits you both."

Susan smiled up at him. She felt none of the hostility she'd expected to feel, only a vague surprise that this man had ever had any hold over her. "Sit down, Tony, you're making the place look untidy just standing there," she said. She turned to Mason. "Order some more drinks, love."

Frank signalled the waiter. "A pint of bitter, an orange juice and . . ."

"I'll have an orange juice, too," Tony said. He saw Susan raise a quizzical eyebrow. "I've stopped drinking since the last time I saw you," he said. "I'm trying to change in a lot of ways."

There was an embarrassed silence for a few seconds which was broken by Frank reaching into his back pocket and pulling out a picture postcard. "This arrived yesterday," he told Tony. "It's from Elsie."

Tony glanced at the picture. "Bloody hell!" he said. "She's in Madeira!"

Mason grinned. "Just couldn't resist rubbing my nose in it, could she?"

"Isn't she worried you'll tell her father where to find her?"

Frank shook his head. "She knows me well enough to be

pretty sure I'd never do that. But even she didn't dare go as far as to tell me who she's living with."

"Who *is* she living with?" Tony asked.

Susan smiled. "Frank has a theory."

"It's more than a theory," Mason said stoutly. "Let's just look at the facts." He began to count them off on the fingers of his right hand. "One: Elsie knew all about the Madeiran job weeks before we pulled it. It was her ideal opportunity to get rid me. All she had to do was have a word with her loving dad, and I'd have been saying hello to the fishes. But she kept quiet about it because she'd already thought of something even smarter she could do. Two: After getting halfway across the Atlantic without any trouble, the *Seaspray* sinks in the English Channel, just a few hundred yards from land."

"There was a storm," Tony pointed out.

"Of course there was a storm," Mason agreed. "Do you really think Nigel would ever have put out to sea if there *hadn't* been one?"

"Frank! Look!" Susan said nervously.

Mason followed the direction of her gaze. Just sitting down at a table a few up from theirs was a hard-looking man in his sixties, flanked by two equally hard, though much younger, men. "I didn't know this was one of Ted Sims' watering holes," he said. He leant across the table and kissed Susan lightly on the cheek. "Don't worry, darlin'."

"You're taking a bit of a chance doing that in front of Ted, aren't you?" Tony asked.

Frank grinned. "*Elsie* left *me*, remember. And Ted's a big enough man to recognise that what's sauce for the goose is sauce for the gander. Anyway, where was I?"

"Three," Susan said.

"Oh yes. Three: Nigel pulls a gun and makes Jack and the other lads get into the tender. Is that sensible? Why would any man in his right mind abandon his crew in the middle of a storm?"

"Because he didn't want them to see who was coming out in the boat to collect the money!" Tony said. "He didn't want them to know it was Linda, instead of you!"

"You're half right," Frank said. "But no more than that. There was a third boat waiting on the coast that night."

"Are you saying . . . ?"

"I think you know exactly what I'm saying," Frank said.

"But there was money washed up on the shore," Tony pointed out.

"A few hundred quid," Frank said dismissively. "Even if they'd sacrificed a few thousand, it wouldn't have mattered. When you think about much money there was altogether, it was only a drop in the ocean." He chuckled at his own unintentional joke.

"So why didn't she shop you to her dad once she'd got what she wanted?" Tony asked. "That way, she could have been sure you wouldn't cause any trouble when she took you for everything you had."

"I've been puzzling over that myself," Frank admitted, "and I've come to the conclusion that, while she's not exactly my biggest fan, she wouldn't wish me any actual harm."

"Ha!" Susan said disbelievingly.

"Then again, maybe she thought that if Ted knew I was behind the job, he'd start to wonder where the money was – and expect a slice of the action himself."

"That's more like it," Susan said.

"Anyway," Frank continued, "she had something else

she could use to keep me in line, didn't she? The photos of us outside the bed-sit. It was much more fun to use them, because that showed just smart she was – and Elsie never could resist the opportunity to show she was brainier then me. 'Course, once I found out how long she'd known about the robbery, I could see just what kind of scam she was pulling."

"Wait a minute!" Tony said. "Are you telling that you knew all about the final double-cross – and you still let her get away with it?"

Frank grinned again. "Well, why not? I had two reasons for pulling the Madeiran job. The first was to prove to myself that I could do it, and the second was because if I pulled it off, I'd be able to get rid of Elsie. So who am I to complain when everything works out – even if it didn't go *exactly* like I planned it."

"Big tough Frank Mason – the softest touch around," Susan said affectionately. "You should thank your lucky stars you've got me to look after you know."

"I do, darlin'," Frank agreed. "I really do."

The waiter arrived with the drinks, but when Frank reached into his pocket he said, "They've already been taken care of by that gentleman over there, sir."

Frank raised his pint glass in Ted Sims' direction. "Cheers, Ted," he mouthed. He turned back to Tony. "Where's Madeira from here?" he asked.

Horton shrugged. "A bit to your right, I think."

Frank swung round in his seat and raised his glass again. "I'd like to make another toast," he said. "Since you're the only man I can think of who would ever have faked his own death to take Elsie off my hands, here's to you, Nigel."